NEVER A DULL MURDER

An Arlie Undercover Cozy Mystery

by

DANI HAVILAND

USA Today Bestselling Author

Copyright

Book Description

How do you solve a murder when there is no weapon, motive, or witness? The case gets more difficult when the Anchorage undercover detective gets 'help' from the victim's friends...
and an adorable bear cub!

(Arlie Undercover Series Book Eight)

CONTENTS

Chapter 1: The Perfect Garden or The Perfect Murder?

"What are you doing here?" Nero asked, tugging off his garden-soil encrusted gloves and tossing them aside. He wiped the excess dirt from his hands on his neon-pink work apron and set his knuckles on his hips, glaring at the man.

"Just came by to say hi to old friend." The dark-haired, pot-bellied man came nearer. "Can I do that?"

"No...no, you can't," Nero stammered and stepped back, unexpectedly overwhelmed by the terror he felt for the first time in a decade. He stumbled on a border block and realized he was being herded into a corner. He had become prey in his own backyard.

Chin up, Nero braced himself, facing the man he had put in prison so many years ago. No, not just a man. He had ratted on his former co-worker in exchange for immunity from prosecution when their operation was discovered.

"I cannot say hi? Why not?" the mustachioed psychopath asked, moving in to close the gap between them. He inhaled deeply and smiled. The acrid smell of fear was intoxicating.

"Because I'm not here and you shouldn't be here either," Nero blurted. He held the man's eyes with his as he felt the front of his apron's deep pockets, searching for a defensive weapon.

Yakov chuckled. He didn't have to see what was going on. He'd be doing the same thing if their places were switched. "I doubt you carry gun while working in flower bed. I see your posies are not up yet." He nodded and grinned. "But you do have very big dahlias in August. Dinnerplate size is name, correct?"

Nero watched Yakov look toward the peonies in bud – the perennial section of his garden – and not where he replanted dozens of his tender dahlias each spring. *Good! He's clueless about me and this place. He must have seen my picture in the Great Gardens of Anchorage article – and hasn't been stalking me since last summer.*

"Dinnerplates, Cactus, Pompom Dahlias – what difference does it make to you, Yakov?" Nero asked, stalling. "I doubt you'll be sticking around to see any of them bloom." *There! It's still in my pocket: my dandelion fork. Not the perfect weapon, but sturdy enough.*

"Why you smile, Sonny? Or do you prefer name Nero? Do pretty little flowers excite you? I remember when other things – how you say? – trip your trigger…" Yakov smirked. "Or have you changed your taste?"

"I only did those things to stay alive. We all did."

Yakov chuffed and shook his head. "Not all of us. Some of us enjoyed it." He inhaled, deeply and dramatically, and his face fell.

Nero's *eau de* fear had disappeared. Testosterone-heavy rage had replaced it. Sonny, his former colleague – the locally famous baker now known as Nero – had returned to his resourceful roots. He could make a weapon out of anything. He reeked of confidence. Yes, he had a plan. Yakov no longer had the upper hand.

Whoosh!

2

Without a second thought, Yakov thrust his weapon into Nero's midsection. Nero stepped aside, though, and pushed his ex-partner backward.

A quick scuffle ensued as the entangled duo each sought dominance. They rolled over each other, each one's top position short-lived. Their clumsy wrestling match rolled across the flower beds, over the wood chip-covered paths, coming to a halt on top of the bleeding hearts plants.

Yakov felt Nero's shoulder tense – he was ready to attack. He reached for his weapon, ready to strike again, but it was gone – lost in the foray. He looked away from Nero's pouty pucker of determination and saw it was still within grasp. But Nero was behaving as if he was now, too.

Diversion time. Yakov bent forward and kissed his former partner hard on the mouth, one hand holding Nero's head, not giving him a chance to turn away. Oh, how he'd wanted to do that for years but had never dared. This was his last chance to feel their joining of warm softness.

Nero gasped, his assault stilled with shock at Yakov's intimate connection.

"Did not expect that, did you?" the intruder hissed as he reached behind him. He grasped his weapon and inhaled, memorizing the scent of the moment, the musky essence of two men's rage and cologne combining, creating a unique aroma.

Yakov stabbed but felt resistance. The heavy fabric of Nero's work apron had blocked the attack. His prey squirmed beneath him as he fumbled with the colorful canvas, attempting to pull it out of the way. Frustrated, Nero stopped trying and threw a clumsy blow to stun his victim.

Nero now dazed, Yakov tugged the apron aside and lunged, thrusting his weapon into the shocked man's midsection. The assault had barely penetrated Nero's thick belly, though. Yakov placed his leather-gloved hands over the end of the slippery tool. He shoved harder, using his body weight to pierce Nero's slightly furry, warm, and creamy skin, forcing the improvised saber deep into his former friend's bowels.

"In the gut. Yes. Slow death for you after what you do to me. No one can blame me for this."

Nero's eyes – wide in terror – blinked in shock. Unable to draw a breath, his mouth formed the single word, "Why?"

"Why I do it or why will they not catch me?"

Yakov watched in glee as his victim tried to speak. Nero's puckered lips opened and compressed in concentration, his eyes squeezed shut, unable to utter even a single word because he couldn't draw a breath.

"I answer for you. I find perfect weapon. It is gone after use." He inhaled deeply and grinned, the fetid smell of Nero's spilled blood and bowels exciting him.

With both the chill of death and his murderer closing in on him, Nero had an epiphany. He still had a choice. He could give Yakov total victory in taking his life or deprive him of the part he enjoyed the most: his victim's agony.

Yakov leaned over and uncurled the dying man from his fetal position, relishing his dominance. He paused, bent closer, and sniffed under Nero's neck, nuzzling his unrequited love's two-day's growth of beard. "The perfect murder," he whispered in his ear.

Nero concentrated on the loss of feeling in his extremities rather than on his pain and impending death. He imagined himself in a glacial lake, the loss of his body's temperature caused by nature's cool waters washing over him rather than his own life bleeding away. A smile crossed his lips.

His last act of revenge would be depriving Yakov of hearing him beg for mercy or watching him suffer.

Confused by Nero's serenity, Yakov scowled. He stood up and nudged him with his boot, then realized what was happening. "You son of a bitch," he hissed, then Nero's body went limp.

His nemesis was dead, an eerie, wide grin of satisfaction frozen on his face.

Forever.

"That not take long enough!" Yakov hissed. He bent over and pulled the body to him, looking closer for signs of life. None. He blew in Nero's face, then licked it. Still no reaction. Dead for sure. "And you don't taste like scared man, either. Damn. Damn. Damn."

Yeo-ow!

Startled by the yowl of a cat, Yakov dropped the body. He quickly looked around, then realized his perfect weapon wasn't a concern. It would be gone by the time Nero was found. Let the local police figure out what happened and who did it.

Payback accomplished.

Perfectly.

CHAPTER 2: To Plan a Wedding
or What a Way to Ruin the Fun

"I think we'll need to rent the convention center if we're going to have a double ceremony," Jess said. "Just on my side, I have lots of friends plus my fellow FBI agents and Deputy US Marshalls. There are also quite a few on the admin side I need to invite so they don't feel alienated."

"Don't forget to invite Arlie," Louie said. "He's not a federal agent but he is a cop." He scratched his head as he thought. "Plus, he's my family. We don't want to just invite law enforcement-type people, either. What about all my bingo partners from the senior center? Oh, and of course, the Senior Security Society...or Symposium or whatever they're calling themselves this week."

"You mean those crazy ladies in capes?" Jess asked with a chuckle. He saw Louie scowl and added, "I meant no disrespect. That's what the crew calls them. Those gals have made quite a name for themselves in the downtown area, making their presence known. Crime is down by fifty percent in some neighborhoods."

"A double ceremony? We appreciate the offer, guys," Tina chimed in. "I'm pretty sure I speak for Rita, too, but don't worry about making it so big. We'd rather have a small event – pretty much just close friends and family plus the officiate. We were thinking of asking Judge Taylor, Arlie's father-in-law, to do the honors."

"Hey, that's who we want to perform our ceremony, too. Are you trying to steal our ideas?" Louie asked.

"Nope," Rita said, popping in from the bedroom where she'd been listening to the whole conversation. "It's just great minds think alike. We might go out to Sleetmute, so Tina's whole family could be a part of it. But at this time of year, everyone's gone – hanging out at fish camps or picking berries."

"That's a bummer," Louie said.

"No, it's not. The ceremony is just to make it legal. We can visit my village whenever we want for a potlatch," Tina said. "Or we can wait until October and have the reception in Anchorage. When the Permanent Fund money comes in, half the Bush comes to the AFN convention."

"What's that?" Louie asked.

"The Bush?" Tina asked, nose wrinkled in disbelief. "That's pretty much any part of the state that's under a thousand people."

"Not that," Louie chuffed. "I mean the other. The ANF."

"That's AFN: Alaska Federation of Natives," Rita replied. "You know, the business meeting they have every year, usually in Anchorage but sometimes in Fairbanks? How long have you lived here?"

"Hey, cut me some slack. If it didn't take place at the Port of Anchorage or in the Eagle River area, I wasn't aware of it. Don't go getting all snooty on me. How would you like it if I…"

Jess put his hand on Louie's shoulder. "Let it go, let it go, let it go…" he sang, his arms now wide like an opera singer as he gave his falsetto impression of the Disney song. He cut short his soliloquy and pulled Louie close. "Words of wisdom from a cartoon character."

"Yeah, well, now I'm not sure if I want a big to-do or not. I've seen those reality shows. I don't want to become a groom-zilla." Louie rubbed a knuckle under his nose, trying to hide his self-consciousness, but it didn't work.

"Hey, hey, hey." Jess gently moved Louie's hand aside and brought his chin up to face him. "How about if we wait until winter? Work won't be so crazy for me then."

"Or maybe a small ceremony like Rita and Tina's?"

Jess grimaced and shrugged. "To be determined. It's our once-in-a-lifetime chance at a total blitz of an event, Louie. Tuxes and tails or tie-dye and do-rags. Food, music, and fun for all, no matter what the attire."

"Now you're starting to sell us on it," Rita said, "or at least me."

"Yeah, me, too," Tina added. "I think we'd better eat first and get some cost estimates before we make any decisions."

"Hey. Didn't you get the memo?" Jess asked, hugging petite Tina across her shoulders. "This one is my treat. Believe it or not, my mother set up a wedding trust fund for me years ago. She was a whiz at investing. The only caveat was that the money could only be used for a wedding. Oh, and that I had to marry before I was forty or it would all go to lost llamas or wayward water buffalos or something. Every time she told me about it, she changed the beneficiary."

"And you're willing to carry us, too?" Rita asked.

"Why not? There's nothing that says the wedding can only be for one couple. As long as I was one of the people getting married, she didn't care. She *did* strongly suggest that I provide an heir within ten years of the marriage but didn't specify I had to marry a woman. I'm not sure if she was that forward-thinking or I was that obvious."

"Or she didn't care one way or the other," Rita said.

"Or she didn't think you'd want to marry a man," Tina added.

"Why don't you ask her?" Louie asked. "I mean, I've never bugged you about her because…" Louie hung his head, unable to voice his last words.

"Because why, Louie?" Jess asked, his hand soft on Louie's back.

"Well, because I never think about us having parents. I know Tina has a mother, but I don't and neither does Rita. And there aren't any fathers around that we care to talk about, either. You're not embarrassed about me, are you?" Louie asked, his face as scarlet as his tee shirt.

"What? No! I love you, you're my fiancé, and I want to marry you in a big way. A HUGE way – with all the trimmings. I want to let everyone know how happy I am. How happy we are. But…"

"But what?" Louie asked.

"I heard she died four years ago. Honestly, though, I think my mother is still alive. I mean, I guess I could look a little harder for her…"

Jess saw a mix of confusion and impending anger on the faces around him. "Let me explain further. You see, when the news reported that her plane had gone down over the Amazon, I made a few phone calls but didn't dig too deep. I accepted the word of the local authorities about it."

Jess shook his head and scowled. "I had to. There was no way I wanted to fly halfway around the world, trudge through the jungle with all those snakes and diseases to…to…" He hissed in frustration.

Tina gritted her molars and glared at her joint forces partner. "You mean you didn't go because you didn't want to deal with mosquitoes?" she growled.

"What? No! I was afraid I'd find her body. Dead. I'd rather believe that she took the opportunity to lay low and was waiting to be declared dead by my stepfather and be done with him, rid of him without a messy divorce. Or maybe she was alive and wanted to come back as someone else. She could have decided to get plastic surgery and pop back in looking like Dolly Parton or Reba McEntire. As long as I *didn't* know for sure what happened, it was possible she was still alive. Right now, I prefer to think she's on an extended search to find her true self."

"Or bring out her inner Dolly," Tina quipped. She met Jess's glare and they both chuckled.

"Or inner Reba," he countered. "She's always wanted to be a redhead. Husband number three gave her so much guff about it, she relented and stayed a brunette. Now that they're separated, he can't tell her what to do. Free at last, Mom, free at last."

"I think that's the most you've ever talked about family," Louie said. "Is that why you're so generous? Because you don't want to be controlling like her husband number three?"

Jess laughed. "He used to get so mad when I'd call him that – Number Three. Well, he was either mad at that or because when I was really ticked, I'd tell him, 'I can't wait until she's done with you. Number Four can't possibly be as big a loser as you.' That would really rile him. But no, I've always been an easygoing sort – as long as no one is taking advantage of someone else, if you know what I mean."

"Yeah," Louie said, "mean people suck, huh? Oh, and that's not a bad word. LuLu's not around anyhow…even if it's a marginal word."

HONK!

All four parents jumped at the sound of the air hour blast.

"Dammit, Winifred!" Louie hollered toward his phone, not bothering to pick it up. "I'm going to get another phone and not give you the number!"

"Don't bother. I'd figure it out before you got a chance to charge the battery for the first time," the leader of the Senior Security Society chuckled.

"I thought you promised not to call me unless it was an emergency," Louie huffed. "And you woke the baby, too."

"It was time for her to get up anyway," Winifred said. "Now, let her mother get her. I need to get in touch with Jess and Tina right away. Someone's just been murdered."

CHAPTER 3: BUSYBODIES 101
OR PLEASE DON'T HELP UNLESS I ASK

"If someone's been murdered, why didn't you call 9-1-1?" Jess asked. He looked at Louie and shrugged a non-verbal, 'Do you mind if I step in?'

Louie nodded assent and stepped away into LuLu's room, joining Rita in rushing their toddler to her potty chair.

"Oh, there you are, Jess. Why didn't you answer your phone?"

"Because, Miss Winifred Pain in the Southern Regions, I left it at my house. It's my day off, and I didn't want to be called in for work when I had personal projects to work on. Again, why didn't you call 9-1-1?"

"Because this person is in the Witness Protection Program. If the call went through the regular channels, the wrong people could find out. Between you, me, and Arlie, we can figure out who did it," she said with conviction.

"How about we leave you and the little old ladies in capes out of this one," Jess said rather than asked. "I'll run over to Arlie's and talk to him face-to-face just in case someone's listening in on his phone."

"Pbbt! His phones are secure. You'll have to find him first, though. He's so deep undercover, no one can find him," Winifred said.

Louie was back and had heard the last part of the conversation. He stifled a giggle. Jess put his finger to his lips and shook his head. Evidently, Winifred didn't know about the bio-trackers that both Arlie and his wife, Charlene, had. Abby – the greatest lab and diagnostics gal in the state of Alaska and maybe the whole USA – could find Arlie even if he was locked in a sea container on a barge in the middle of the Pacific Ocean…and had!

"So," Jess began slowly, trying to make sure he chose his words carefully, "you need help with someone's murder but can't call Anchorage PD or the FBI?"

"I *did* just call the FBI, didn't I?" Winifred sassed.

"No, you called Louie. And as far as I know, he's not a part of any law enforcement agency – municipal, state, or federal."

"That's true, but he may have a vested interest in this, shall we call it, situation."

Jess blinked away a myriad of fears and anxieties about his fiancé who was also in Witness Protection and asked. "Where do you want to meet?"

"The scene of the crime. Louie, your favorite baker has bit his final biscuit. I'm here at his home now. Don't dawdle."

The screen went blank.

Jess looked at Louie. "I hope you know where she's talking about because I sure as heck don't."

"Yeah, I do. Let me jump the fence and see if Charlene knows where Arlie is. I don't want to ask Abby to track him if I don't have to. Besides, her line might be bugged."

Jess started to roll his eyes at the thought that a line from the Anchorage Crime Lab might be bugged, then realized anything was possible. "Yeah, go ahead. I'll get my gear."

He turned to the women. Rita was on the couch, hugging LuLu close, rocking her back and forth, letting the toddler awaken from her nap slowly. "It looks like it's just you ladies here this afternoon. Too bad, too. I was all set to put together a barbecue."

"Do you want me to come along with you?" Tina asked. "I am part of the Anchorage Police Department, after all."

Jess shook his head. "I have to trust that Winifred has a valid reason not to ask you. I'd say it was for plausible deniability. Arlie can get by with doing a lot of marginal 'stuff' because he's undercover. You're a rookie and need to play by *all* the rules."

Tina snorted. "I'm a team player, but I can also bend the rules into a pretty bow if needed."

"I don't doubt it, Tina, but I'd rather Rita wasn't alone with LuLu. There's safety in numbers. Then again, this whole alert might just be the delusions of a little old retired police academy teacher. Who knows?"

"Better safe than sorry, right?" Rita asked. "We'll be fine, Jess. As a matter of fact, I think I'll get started on a potato salad and maybe some coleslaw. Give us a shout when you're twenty minutes away, and we'll fire up the grill. The steaks are already thawed and will be seasoned soon."

"Save the slaw for kielbasa and go for a green instead of potato salad if you don't mind." Jess turned to Tina. "Take care of my girls, all right?"

"You know I will. Take care of yourself and Louie, too. I'm not psychic but something stinks about this whole deal. As twisty-turny as

I can bend around regulations, this is a little too off the books for me. It stinks like a setup."

"Don't worry. I'm recording everything once I'm out the door. Arlie set me up with a real cool hat." He took a baseball cap off the hat rack by the door.

"Seattle Seahawks?" Tina asked. "I've never known you to wear any sports-related gear much less a baseball cap."

"This is more like 'See' hawks," Jess said, holding the hat closer to look for telltale inconsistencies. "Once it's activated, it automatically notifies Abby that it's live and in use. It uploads both audio and video to the cloud in real time, too."

"That's cool, but it'd be nicer if it had a biometric device to make sure the wearer's heart's still ticking, too," Tina said.

"It does," Jess whispered in her ear. "Another Arlie creation, monitored by Abby."

"You'd better get going before Louie finds out about it. He'll want one, too."

"Don't worry about him. I'll keep him close. We still have a wedding to plan."

***

"Just up there," Louie said, pointing to the end of the cul-de-sac. "The back of his place opens out to the greenbelt. After that, it's national forest. I think Sonny – I mean, Nero – must have had some pretty good information to be gifted that chunk of prime real estate."

"If Sonny-er-Nero is who I think he is, he did. He went dark before my time. If he's lasted this long, it's a credit to someone on our side or an insult to the bad guys."

"We never talked about it. But, um…" Louie paused and looked to Jess. "Now we're going to have to have someone else do the catering for our wedding."

"He was a caterer? That's about the riskiest…" Jess slammed his open hand on the steering wheel, the day's frustrations catching up to him.

Louie put his hand on Jess's shoulder to calm him. "He wasn't ours or anyone else's caterer, but he was the guy I wanted to bake the rolls and some of the *horse divorces*. He probably could bake a nice cake but that wasn't his specialty. He made the best sourdough bread in the world. And he never had a store. He only sold to wholesalers and that was through a third party. See?" Louie pointed to a chimney, smoke coming out of it despite the balmy seventy-degree weather.

Jess got out of the car and waited for Louie to join him. "Yeah, so the guy had a fireplace. Lots of people use them all year round."

"Not at this time of day, they don't. Besides, that's not a fireplace. It's a brick oven for his breads and pastries. His galettes are worth dying for. Oops. That was the wrong thing to say. I mean, they're real, real good."

The two walked around the house to the backyard. "Well, it looks like Winifred found Arlie," Jess said, nodding to the pair deep in conversation.

"Nope. I did," Louie said. "I told him to contact her."

Jess squinted at Louie and the story changed slightly. "Okay. I *asked* Arlie to contact her," Louie said. "He told me this might be the break he was looking for."

"There's my man," Winifred called out to Louie, her face bright with honest joy. She looked at Jess and scowled at his Seahawks hat, then over at Louie who was bare headed. She reached into her bag and pulled out a baseball cap.

"Wrong team, Jess," she said. "Louie, wear one of these Chinooks caps. Support the home team. Besides, redheads need more protection from the sun. Where's yours, Arlie? I have more."

"Let's stay on task, shall we, ma'am?" Arlie said. "I work in the shadows enough that I shouldn't need one. If I do, I have one in the car. Now, how did you find out about this? Oh, and I assume nothing's been touched, and the body hasn't been moved."

"Yes, on the latter. I couldn't have moved him if I tried." She patted her metallic-red scooter. "Old Ruby has fat, foam-filled tires, but she doesn't care to go off road. Or off trail. How I found out about him? I guess it was pure dumb luck."

"Ma'am, you never operate on dumb luck," Arlie said.

"We're not at the academy, Arlie. You can call me Winifred."

Arlie – still intimidated by his mentor – opened his mouth to say, "Yes, ma'am," then quickly shut it and nodded. "Dumb luck or otherwise, what time did you get here? And why didn't you call downtown and report it?"

"My phone ran out of battery after I called Louie, looking for Jess. I didn't call 9-1-1 because I was pretty sure this property was on national park property and therefore it would be a federal case. That, and I knew Nero was in the Witness Protection Program."

"I've never known you not to have at least two backup batteries, Winifred. And you're right about it being on park land. Still, I could use my team's help to look for evidence. It looks like there was a fight before he went down." He sniffed and frowned. "Gut wound."

"I can smell the stink, but how can you tell there was a fight first?" Louie asked. "His face isn't all beat up."

"But his back is filthy. Unless he rolled down a hill and came to a stop here, it wouldn't have gotten that dirty."

Arlie stooped beside the body and looked at the hands of the corpse, the fisted white knuckles unmarked. "It looks like it was more of a wrestling than boxing match. He must have been working in the yard when he was attacked. Even if he lost his balance, he wouldn't have rolled over repeatedly. And he wouldn't have trashed his pride and joy – his garden – on purpose."

"Especially his favorite flowers," Winifred added. "Those bleeding hearts will come back next year, but he was passionate about everything he grew out here. 'My little bit of Eden' he'd call it."

"Well," Jess squatted at the edge of the bark-covered pathway, "it looks like the other man in the scuffle was heavy set, had a limp, and really didn't care if he got caught or not."

"Why do you say that?" Arlie asked. "I mean, I got the first two from his footprints, but why didn't he care?"

"He threw his gloves away." Jess pointed to them. Black leather gloves had been casually tossed aside, nearly invisible next to a black plastic bag of garden debris.

"How do you know they belong to the murderer?" Louie asked.

19

"Couldn't they be Nero's?"

"Nope," Arlie said, agreeing with Jess's conclusion. "Those are high-dollar gloves. They don't belong around dirt. If they had been Nero's, he would have left them in the house, or at least somewhere away from all this dirt and mud."

"Probably true," Winifred said. Her chin lifted and tone changed as she added smugly, "It's kind of hard to get prints off the inside of leather, but it can be done. I know because I've done it before."

"Yes, I remember," Arlie said, crouching beside the gloves. He stuck a pencil into the first one, inspected it, and put it in an evidence bag. He did the same to the second one, this time grinning before he stowed it in another baggie. "But the fact that he was so cavalier in disposing of them, I'd say he knew we wouldn't find the murder weapon."

"You don't kill someone by shooting or stabbing them in the gut and not have a weapon." Jess saw Arlie's smirk and added, "What? Do you think he used a light saber?"

"Too much blood for something like that," Arlie replied. "A laser would have cauterized the wound right away and staunched the blood flow."

"Maybe someone shot him with ice bullets?" Louie suggested.

"Ice bullets? Now that's just ridiculous," Winifred scolded. "How can you fire a projectile of ice and not have it melt completely by the time it left the muzzle? Now you're just spewing nonsense."

"You could if it was dry ice," Louie argued. "That stuff's really, really cold. I mean, like if you froze a person's hand with it, someone

20

could smash it with a hammer, and it'd shatter!"

"You watch too many superhero movies, Louie," Winifred said.

"No, I don't. Well, not now that I have a little girl." Louie rolled his eyes. "Lately all we've been watching are princesses and ponies. That's where I saw frozen people being smashed to pieces, too."

Bzzz.

Even though the humming wasn't much louder than a mosquito, all eyes looked up for it.

"And there's my team," Arlie said. He put his two fingers to his cheek and asked, "Are you almost here?"

Abby replied, "Only my eyes and ears. The rest of me is stuck at the bottom of the hill. You know how it is. In Alaska, there are two seasons, winter and…"

Arlie chuckled and took the bait, "And construction. Just get here when you can. I'll make sure there's a path cleared to the backyard. I'll get everyone back so Buzz can get his pictures."

"*Her* pictures," Abby corrected. "Oh, and I see Winifred's trying to get back in the game. Watch what you say around her. The hat she gave Louie is almost the same as Jess's See Hawk cap."

"Yeah, that hat Louie's wearing is kinda cute, isn't it." Arlie looked up at the small but powerful drone overhead. "We'll see you when you get here, Abby," he said, this time directing his voice toward the drone but still speaking to her through the synthetic mole behind his ear. "Bye for now."

Chapter 4: I Spy from the Sky
or See-Hawks and Chinook Looks

"Is that the new brainiac contraption Abby built?" Louie asked. His eyes followed the camo-gray strider spider in the sky as it sped into the yard, then hovered over the corpse.

"She and I created that little sweetheart together," Arlie said, smirking in pride.

Jess chuckled and smacked him on the back. "You and Abby built a baby together? Congratulations!"

Arlie laughed in surprise. "I'm not her type and you know it. We shared the same vision, though. We both have specialized skills and wed them to create Buzz."

"What'll it do?" Louie asked. "Oh, wait. I'm not supposed to know, huh? Don't mind me. As long as we can find out who killed Nero, I'll be happy. Well, sort of. Now that he's gone, we don't have anyone to make appetizers and sourdough mini baguettes. Damn, I mean, darn!"

Arlie elbowed his pouty friend and whispered, "You just have to change your perspective, Louie. Think of all the fun you'll have taste-testing breads and *hors de oeuvres* from prospective bakers." He looked at Jess for the answer in his eyes. "You still have a few weeks before the wedding, right?"

A wide smile spread across Louie's face and his eyes brightened with anticipation. "Oh, yeah. That's right. LuLu can help me, too.

Thanks, Arlie. You always seem to know the right thing to say."

Arlie glanced up at Buzz, the aerial contraption pivoting in place in seemingly spastic pauses as it scanned the scene of the crime with a dozen different sensors and cameras. "She's a beauty, Abby," he said softly, knowing she'd hear him through his freckle-colored communicator.

"Yeah, she is," Abby replied, suddenly at his side.

An immediate, short-lived tension in his shoulders was the only outward indication that Abby had startled Arlie. "Oh, hi there, Abby. I didn't see you come in."

"You know, one of these days I'll be able to sneak up on you and make you squeal."

"I don't squeal," Arlie said dryly.

"Yes, you do," Louie chimed in. "At least, you do when Charlene sneaks up on you."

"Well, that's different. You'd squeak, too, if you were both startled and goosed at the same time."

"Yeah, I guess I would," Louie said, grinning at Jess. "I mean, I do." He looked around. "Where did Winifred go? She was just here. She can't move that fast in her electric scooter."

"I'm over here, Louie," Winifred called out from a dark corner of the garden. "That little spy in the sky can do a lot of things, but it can't sniff out a trail like a good tracking dog."

Arlie winked at Abby who kept her smug smile of maternal pride turned away from the senior citizen investigator. "Can *you*, Winifred?" Arlie asked. "I mean, are you part bloodhound or beagle or something?"

"Or something," she replied and grunted, leaning forward to push a dandelion leaf aside with her claw-handled grabber.

Camo-gray Buzz came over and hovered above the weed, too. The aerial device paused briefly between jerky rotations, using her wide spectrum of sensors to measure the botanical and chemical compounds, also recording the relative humidity and temperature of the ground Winifred was exposing.

"What did you find?" Arlie asked.

Winifred cut her eyes to him, then glanced at Abby. "What? Didn't that oversized mosquito tell you already, or can it?"

"Yes, *she* can," Abby said. "Arlie and I just want to know if you came to the same conclusion."

"It's just a dandelion," Winifred said, returning the grabber to the scooter's basket. "The weed is too far away from the victim to be important, but it wasn't trampled like most of the other plants in the yard. I thought it might be significant."

"So, does this mean you're done here, Winifred?" Arlie asked.

"Why do you ask?"

"Because I have a body to remove. I don't want unnecessary people in the area. I know you're tough and very adaptable, but I don't think you'd be as much help to me as Jess with loading Nero onto the gurney."

Winifred looked around, ready to make a comment about Louie and Abby also being there, then noticed they had already left and were standing in the driveway. "Then I guess it's time for me to leave, too."

Arlie put his hand on her shoulder as she started to back up. "Thanks for the call. If you get any gut suspicions, let me know. That's something our electronic gizmos can never enhance or recreate."

"Oh, and thanks for the hat, Winifred," Louie said, waving his Chugiak-Eagle River Chinooks baseball cap. "I'll see you at bingo on Friday."

Winifred rolled her eyes, then chuckled. "You got it." *Maybe it really is time to retire and let the next generation take over the investigations. Bingo, crossword puzzles, and old TV reruns seem to be all the future I have now.*

***

"I think you hurt her feelings," Jess whispered to Arlie as they stood over the corpse, finished with the photos they had taken of Nero in his found position.

"No, she's tougher than that. I think she suspects something and doesn't want to share the information. I wouldn't be surprised if she called us here because she and Nero were having an affair, and that's why she found him."

"Her? Winifred the Iron Maiden? Having a fling? I can't imagine her even having a flirt," Jess said in a harsh whisper.

"Look up her file if you have the clearance. She was an American Mata Hari in her day. More than one Russkie was willing to give up his secrets for a little of her attention."

"If you say so…" Jess turned his full attention to helping Arlie remove the body. He pulled the dead man's shoulder forward and tried to get a hand under him.

Arlie did the same thing, but it was slow going. After a half dozen lifts and tugs and as many grunts, the body was moved onto the gurney.

"I wonder why he's smiling?" Jess asked. "I've never seen a victim of a violent death do that."

Arlie chuffed. "I'd say to piss off his murderer. I know I wouldn't give anyone trying to kill me the satisfaction of seeing fear on my face or hearing me beg."

"Yeah, I guess I'd be the same way. I'm lucky that I've never been in that situation."

"Well, Jess, let's hope you die a virgin that way."

"Huh?"

"That you never face someone trying to kill you." Arlie shook his head, flashes of vivid and vile memories momentarily overwhelming him.

"Oh, I've faced a few tough guys but only in situations that I knew were balanced in my favor. It looks like Nero didn't have much of a chance."

"There's always a chance, Jess. It's just that sometimes the odds are very, very slim."

"If you're done..." Abby said, breaking into their philosophical discussion of facing dire circumstances or death.

"Yes," they drawled and looked towards her.

"Would you put him in the van and make sure the door is

locked?"

"Why?" Jess asked. "Are you afraid someone's going to try and steal your corpse?"

"Nope," Abby answered. "I don't want to tempt the neighborhood kids, though."

Jess looked at Arlie for an explanation. "That's right," Arlie said. "You haven't seen her *discreet* coroner's wagon, have you. She can pull in anywhere and not raise suspicions."

"What do you mean?"

Arlie laughed as Abby deadpanned, "Because it's disguised as an ice cream truck."

"Oh, geez… Give me a break."

"Not yet. We have to get Nero wrapped and stashed first." Arlie turned to Abby. "Do you have it with you or do I have to fetch it from your Sweet Sprinkles Sundae Sedan?"

"Hey! That name almost works, but it's not quite right. Yes, I brought the shroud. Here," Abby handed him a purple tie-dye backpack trimmed in neon green.

"Are you sure that bag's bright enough?" Jess teased.

Arlie unzipped the top and pulled out a shrink-wrapped rectangle. "That's part of its charm. If this wee bag is stolen, it'd be hard to hide. Not only the bright purple but the green trim is luminescent. It's designed to shine when it's left in pitch black darkness unless the access code is activated." He tore open the package he'd retrieved and shook out what looked like a drop cloth with lettering. "Here, grab an end and help me spread it over him."

Jess read the print aloud, "Warning: Contents may be toxic." He grunted in disapproval. "And you're putting this body in an ice cream truck?"

Arlie unfolded it the rest of the way, then pulled the bright orange tab.

Whoosh!

"What in the hell was that?" Jess asked, jumping back at the sudden noise, dropping the blanket.

"Yeah, what he said," Louie echoed, clutching his fiancé's arm.

The three men watched as the cloth expanded, creating an airy covering with a puff-quilted configuration.

Abby giggled. "You can't let people know that you're removing a person. This disguises the shape. See." She stuck her hand under an edge, causing the area to fold over like the corner of a box. "You can't tell what's under here, can you?"

Jess and Louie shook their heads in tandem.

Arlie reached into the backpack and pulled out two more packets. "Bear or moose?" he asked Abby.

"Probably bear," Abby replied. "He's too short and chunky to be a moose."

"Huh?" Louie asked.

Arlie put away one pack and opened the other. "Watch this. Instant bear claws, complete with foot and leg."

"Ew!" Jess and Louie groaned.

Abby spread the shape-hiding blanket over the corpse, then lifted a corner and attached the *faux* bear leg to the gurney. "Looks like we're hauling off a dead bear, doesn't it?" she asked the pair.

"Pretty clever," Jess said.

"But you're putting it in an ice cream truck," Louie said.

"A second-hand ice cream truck with the name spray-painted out," Arlie explained. "It's now repurposed as a hearse. Plus, it really was an ice cream truck. Abby needs refrigeration to keep the body chilled until she can perform an autopsy."

"Assist in an autopsy," Abby said. "I just watch and take samples. I leave the heavy-duty stuff to the professionals. Haul him away!"

"You sure seem cheery about this, Abby," Louie said. "Do you really like your job that much?"

"Yes, I do, Louie. Catching bad guys is Arlie and Jess's job. Pointing them in the right direction is mine."

***

A half-hour earlier

Yakov watched from behind the dumpster across the street. His nose twitched in disgust. Evidently, someone had cleared out their freezer in anticipation of fishing season. The stench would only get stronger as the day went on. He swatted at a large, overwintered mosquito as it flew by his face, then froze.

A gold minivan pulled up in front of Nero's house and stopped.

Nero had company.

The engine shut off, but no one got out.

Click. Errr. Clack.

Yakov listened to the mechanical noises, then watched as the lift gate at the back of the van descended. An old woman on a metallic-red scooter backed out, her back straight and proud as if she was the queen of the neighborhood.

Yakov's heart raced momentarily. *Hope snoopy woman not doctor person. Hmph. It does not matter. Nero has fatal wound. Whether dead now or not, that grinning S.O.B. could not have more than one hour left in him. As warm as today is, any evidence remaining is gone. After woman go, I go, too.*

CHAPTER 5: BEAR CLAWS
OR SPUMONI?

"Damn his hide," Winifred cursed softly as she drove into her driveway. "I told him to be more careful." She pushed the button on the minivan's overhead console and the garage door opened.

"And damn me for not being more insistent."

After half a minute of fumbling with the buttons on her keychain fob, Winifred got out of her handicapped-adaptive van. She maneuvered her ruby-red scooter in tight circles, around the tail end of the vehicle, and into her house. "And damn me again for not stepping up to get that experimental surgery. Right now, I'd give just about anything to be able to walk again, to catch Nero's killer, and kick some serious ass. Damn, damn, damn!"

Unexpected tears burst out. "Where's your tough skin now, Lady Ironsides?" She pulled a handkerchief from her purse and anxiously dabbed at the dribbles under her nose.

"Oh, what the hell! Go ahead and give it a good honking, woman. No one's around to hear you blow your nose like a camper."

More tears flowed as she remembered Nero – the felon once known as Sonny – in his younger years. Barely five-six, he had shoulders as broad as a man a foot taller. She always was a sucker for a lumberjack's body.

Her Sonny had never been a lumberjack, though. 'I care too much for plants to fell one,' he told her the last time she'd found him. "Look at this yard. Have you ever seen anything so verdant? I even let a few dandelions grow. I don't care if they're weeds. They're the first flowers to bloom each spring."

Sniff, sniff.

"My Sonny. My Nero. It only took me two years to find you after the Witness Protection relocated you this time," she said. "Four times they moved you, but I always found you."

She huffed in self-derision. "But it took nearly fifteen years to get up the nerve to say hi. I took it as fate or kismet or whatever that they moved you just a few miles away. You were gone from my radar for three more years, then one taste of that sourdough bread, and I knew I'd found you."

Winifred wheeled over to her chest freezer. She reached in and grabbed one of the last loaves of bread he'd baked. "'These are just for you,' you said. 'The perfect size for a meal for the both of us.'"

She held the mini loaf close to her chest and sobbed anew.

Grief.

She'd never had it so deep.

"Now I know why lovers weep so much. It isn't so much the loss of joy – the warmth and comfort of your other half – as it is its replacement with icy shards of anguish. A void would be easier to bear."

Winifred unzipped the plastic bag and sniffed the bread. "I'll let you warm up first. Oh, I am so going to find your killer, Nero. Gone too soon, love. Gone too soon."

***

Enroute to coroner's office

Abby bore the stop-and-go traffic of the early summer tourist season with minimal cursing. "Why does the morgue and all the other ghoulie government sites have to be located mid-town? And why can't the governor or mayor or whoever establish a tourist-proof route for locals? Something that doesn't show up on a GPS, so people who live and work here don't get bogged down with Lookie Lous."

She swiped the side of her smart sunglasses, cranking up the volume of the vintage grunge band playing through the earpieces. "At least I have good tunes to keep me company." She looked over her shoulder and through the glass to the refrigerated section of the box truck. "You wouldn't like my music anyhow, Nero. You seem like the kind of guy who'd listen to long-hair music. And I mean Tchaikovsky, not The Rolling Stones. Then again, maybe Guns 'N Roses were more your style."

She chuckled. "I'm my own best company at times. At least, I have thick skin. We'll find out soon enough what you were made of. Stabbed in the gut is a miserable way to die. Someone really must have hated you, dude."

Abby flinched as the phone call came through her glasses, interrupting her favorite guitar riff. "Hey, Manny! I'm getting there as fast as I can. You know how it is. Give me about…" She paused, then honked the horn as she pulled around the back of the building, up to the secure garage entrance. "Two seconds."

"You know, I knew you were close," Manny said. "I swear I could hear the whining of your music from here."

"Not possible," she said and tapped the side of her glasses, disconnecting their phone call. "I gave up on full throttle speakers a long time ago."

Manny bit back his frustration at her subtle putdown and walked around the back of the repurposed ice cream truck. "What flavor did you bring me today? Chocolate or Vanilla or maybe Caramel Cream?"

Manny heard the click of the lock mechanism as she pushed the button. He pulled open the door and screeched, "Geez, woman! Since when did you make call outs to pick up roadkill? And a bear at that!"

She playfully picked up the *faux* leg and bit into the end of it. "What? I thought you liked bear claws. Mmm!"

"That's disgusting."

"No, it's shaped vinyl with glued-on polyester strands to take away the shine." Abby sputtered, spitting out a fake hair. "Not chocolate or vanilla but maybe spumoni. He looks Italian. Lots of dark hair everywhere but on the top of his head."

Manny lifted a corner of the inflatable cover and gasped at the body. "Geez! That's the biggest mustache I've ever seen. Hey, why in the heck is he smiling?"

"That's the second question."

"What's the first?" Manny replaced the shroud.

"What murder weapon was used?" She held up the two baggies with a glove in each. "Maybe we can find a hint on these, but I doubt it. One thing's for sure, it was a professional hit. This guy was supposed to be off everyone's radar."

"It only takes one, Abby. Just one person is all that's needed to screw up your Witness Protection identity."

Manny wrangled the gurney to the end of the van and released all four wheeled-legs on the base. "I can take it from here," he said. "Oh, and what's his name? I assume with a mustache like that, he's a guy."

"I didn't check beneath the belt, but let's call him Smiley for now."

"You don't know who he is?"

"Nope. I know who's house he was at, but that doesn't mean he was the homeowner. I'll get prints and verify. You just get him on the table. Don't start without me. I'll be right back."

Abby pulled her knees together and rolled her eyes, then rushed out of the loading area into the ladies' room. She looked down the hall and made sure she was alone, then locked herself into the lavatory. "Alex, call Arlie," she said.

Her smart glasses connected the call. "Hey, Arlie. Who knows what's going on besides you, me, Jess, Louie, and Winifred?"

"That's it. Why?"

Abby shuddered. "Nothing I can put a finger on. At least, not yet."

"Did you get those shivers you always get when something isn't right?"

"Yeah, I did, and I still have them."

"Me, too," Arlie said. "And Louie makes three. He said the same thing."

"Gotta go. Manny's waiting for me to start the autopsy. I'll call you later."

"Okay. Later, then."

Abby patted water on her face, dried it, then threw the paper towel in the trash. "Hmph. Too bad the willies didn't wash off, too." She shivered again and looked around the restroom. "Quit that, ghost! I'll find your killer, I promise. You have to stop distracting me, though."

The lights flickered as she opened the door into the hall. A sudden peace washed over her. "Thanks," she said. "Now let's get started."

Thump, thump, thud, crash!

Abby raced into the lab at the sound of chaos. Manny was sprawled out on the floor next to the corpse, a tangle of inflatable blanket and fake bear legs, his white lab coat askew. One of his legs kicked out as he struggled to stand up.

"What in the hell?" he grunted and pushed the dead body off him.

Abby offered her hand to help him to his feet. "What happened?"

"I don't know. One minute I'm pushing the gurney away from the van, the next it feels like I'm getting tackled." He looked down at the front of his pants. "Oh, thank God."

"What?"

"I was afraid I'd pissed myself," he said with a nervous chuckle. "I never believed in ghosts until now."

"Do you think…" Abby stammered, trying to remember the nickname she'd given him. She looked at the corpse and chuckled in recall. "Smiley. Do you think Smiley jumped you?"

"Noo," Manny drawled, "but I think his ghost might have."

"Enough about ghosts. Let's get moving before you give me the jitters, too. We're trained professionals. Science – not seances and Tarot cards – will give us answers."

Manny took a deep breath, straightened his lab coat, and pasted on an exaggerated smile of confidence. "We got this. I guess I'd better lay off coffee in the afternoon. I can't afford an…a screwup."

Abby looked down at the floor so he couldn't read her face. She knew he was about to say, 'another screwup.' It was common knowledge that he'd transferred to Alaska from Chicago. He'd messed up big time, and it was either transfer to a small town or lose his license. His talents were too good to waste on Dimweed, South Dakota. The remoteness of Alaska and the big city of Anchorage was the compromise.

"You got this, Manny."

He nodded, now more confident.

"Then point me to the PPE." She flashed her app-laden smartphone at him. "I'm ready to assist."

Three minutes later, geared up with apron, mask, and gloves, Abby stood by the exam table. "This isn't going to work." She picked up a towel and set it gently over the dead man's face. "I can't have a corpse smiling at me while you're cutting into him."

"Thanks," Manny said. "If you hadn't done it, I would have."

The two worked together well, Abby anticipating Manny's need for the tools of the trade. Just as he opened his mouth to say, "Scalpel," she handed it to him.

Occasionally, she watched him, taking her focus away from the job. With his mask, she couldn't see his mouth, but Manny's eyebrows said a lot. He was more intent than she'd ever seen him before. She'd only known him a few weeks, but this was their second – no, their third – autopsy together. Normally, she didn't do hands on, preferring to work with test results and numbers, not her fingers.

Manny paused and looked up at her – as if he could feel her eyes on him – and grinned.

"What?" she asked.

"I didn't say anything."

"Oh. It must have been a gust of wind."

"Abby, we're inside a sealed lab, in the middle of a concrete building. No wind in here."

"Yeah. You're right." She reached up and pushed her bangs out of her face with the back of her gloved hand. "This is a little intense. Ten minutes at this seems like ten hours."

"Only because there's nothing obvious. Searching for answers takes a lot more energy than finding and interpreting them. Answers, that is. Besides, we're almost done here."

Abby grunted an assent, then faced away, suddenly uncomfortable with her co-worker.

Manny waited for her to look back, making sure he could see the answer in her eyes. "Do you want to go grab a bite to eat with me?"

"Um, no."

"Oh, do you still get squeamish around dead bodies?" he joked, then winked at her.

Her response was a wide-eyed, 'What are you talking about?'

blank expression.

He sobered up and changed his approach. "Okay, then how about we have a drink or three? You know, drink some Forget-Me-Not cocktails, and see what pops up."

Still confused, this time Abby asked, "Huh?"

He winked at her. "You know…pops up?"

"Pops up?" Confusion evaporated as she caught his teasing hip gyration. "Oh, no, no, no! I mean, I'm married."

"I won't tell if you don't."

"No, you don't understand. I don't date co-workers."

"So, we only work on special assignments together. We're in different departments, so therefore not co-workers."

Abby pulled down her mask and looked him in the eye. "I. Don't. Date. Men."

Manny chuckled nervously. "Huh? Oh! Well, maybe you just haven't found the right guy."

She brought her mask back up and shook her head. "And maybe you haven't either. Nope, not interested. Let's get him stitched back together. I'm beat and ready to get out of here. My day started early."

"You go ahead," Manny said, a tinge of apology in his voice. "I got this."

"Are you sure?"

"Yup. Oh, and sorry about the pass. It was inappropriate."

"Yeah, it was. Don't worry, though. I won't say anything. You owe me one, though."

"Tell your wife she's lucky," Manny said, winking.

Abby forced her growl into a chuckle. "No concerns there. Believe me, she knows it."

She turned away and her sour demeanor returned. She quickly shucked her PPE gear, tossed it in the trash, and was out the door and into the solitude of the garage in a hurry. When she spotted the ice cream truck, inner peace returned and comforted her.

Her new project.

The request for a discreet portable science lab had been turned down, but a used transport vehicle could be squeezed into the budget. The new, upgraded equipment installed into her lab downtown was wonderful, but often on-site analyses were time critical, evidence literally evaporating before it could be sent to Anchorage. Buzz the Drone's sensors could only detect a certain type of data. Microscopes and spectrometers were still needed for old-fashioned sleuthing.

"Indescribably Delicious Eats," she said aloud, running her hand across the side of the truck. She opened the driver's door. "Nah. I don't want a crowd of kids around while I'm working."

Once inside, she started the engine. "Alaska Roadkill Meats and Sausages? Hmm. Sounds promising but still needs work."

The automatic garage door opened as she approached it, letting her out into the bright, early summer sunshine. Her smart glasses immediately darkened. "Time for more tunes before getting to the office and comparing Manny's autopsy notes and data with mine and Buzz's. Hopefully, something will line up."

"Eek!"

Abby lurched forward and slammed on the breaks, unsure if it was her or someone else who had screeched in fright. She took off her glasses and looked for smudges. Had she seen something, too?

Chapter 6: A Girl Has to Go or He Has to Go

Because of construction-related traffic delays and detours, it took Abby ten minutes to drive two miles to her lab downtown. She pulled into the secure underground garage and shut off her tunes, grateful for the distraction of the heart-pumping strains of Bohemian Rhapsody. She shifted emotional gears into solving the mysteries of the day and picked up her drone from the passenger seat.

"No reason to run down your battery, Buzz," she said as she headed to the stairwell, the drone cradled in her arms. "We're both going to the same place. It's cool to hitch a ride with me."

Chirp.

"You're talking to me now?" she asked, shocked at the response from the unit.

Chirp.

"What the heck…?"

"It's not her, it's me," Arlie said, opening the security door to let her in. "It's just a little something I added to your program. I couldn't access the hardware to install a voice chip. The low battery alarm was already there, so I tapped into that."

"Are you messing with my girl?" Abby asked, giving him an impish scowl.

"Sort of. And she's *our* girl. I just wanted to have an audible in case something came up. How about one chirp to get your attention, two chirps for no?"

"One chirp for yes or hi, two chirps for no, and three chirps for 'get the heck out of there,'" Abby suggested. "I mean, she is our creation. I want a say in her voice, too."

"Well, until we get some downtime and can give her a sound box, that should do." Arlie changed topics, "So, what did you find out from the new guy in the coroner's office? His name's Manny, right?"

"I found out he's an incorrigible flirt. I don't know what he did to get transferred to the morgue in Anchorage from his cushy job back east, but I don't doubt there's at least a sexual harassment charge or three in his personnel file."

Arlie chuckled. "I'm sure you put him in his place."

"Yeah, but I'd rather have given him a black eye or bloody nose. Lazy son of a biscuit eater. Can't even prowl the nightclubs or bars for a date – he does it while at work where the women can't run away."

"You can file charges."

"I'd rather let him off with a warning. But don't worry. He's not getting off easy. I'll spread the word about what a slimeball he is to all the ladies in the building."

"How are you going to do that? Last I knew, you stayed pretty much holed up in your lab."

"Arlie, a girl still has to go, you know." Abby squeezed her knees together and frowned. "Notes taped to the back of the stall doors plus one on the mirrors in both buildings should do it. That kind of warning isn't easily forgotten."

Abby cuddled the drone close and stepped back, so Arlie could let them in. "There wasn't anything special about it, though. Nero's was a usual 'hum drum, cut, and collect' autopsy. Manny seemed more interested in me than the procedure. That part was very irritating. I started to point out the configuration of the stab wound but he was already cutting elsewhere. So, I just took a few extra pictures of my own instead. He'll submit his photos and findings with the final report. I'll have mine, too."

Abby handed Buzz to Arlie, tapped her ID card on the sensor, and opened her lab. Arlie set Buzz down on the first flat surface he saw and waited for Abby to continue. She pulled out her phone and handed it to him. "Look at these."

Arlie swiped through the latest photos, stopping when he got to a selfie Abby had taken of herself in skimpy lingerie. "Oops. Too far," and went back to the images of the deep, round puncture wound in Nero's flabby belly.

"Not a traditional cutting edge on the murder weapon then," he said. "Maybe an awl?"

"It would have had to be industrial-sized and would have left traces of metal, ceramic, or plastic." Abby stood close and zoomed into the area in question.

"The wound would have collapsed as soon as it was pulled out, too. Plus, we never found the weapon. The assailant must have taken it with him. There's no way it wasn't covered in blood. No trail leading away from the body, either."

"He must have had a cloth or bag with him," Arlie suggested.

"Don't you hate tidy murderers?" Abby chuckled. "Nah, why

would he do that? It wasn't his DNA spewed all over the place but that of the victim."

"But there wasn't a mess other than what was on Nero...and barely any under his body. Have you analyzed Buzz's data?"

"Arlie, when would I have had the time? I drove straight to the autopsy, and then came here."

"You're good at multitasking, Abby. Maybe you figured out how to have the data read out to you. You could listen to it with those fancy glasses of yours. I don't think anything is beyond your ability."

"Ah, that's sweet... But no. Give me an hour to see which road I'll take."

"Excuse me?" Arlie asked. "Are you going somewhere?"

"Nope. By which road, I mean which spectrum has the most interesting data. I think I'll check the gas analysis first. We haven't been able to collect that in the field before. Who knows, maybe the murderer's pheromones are unique, and Buzz captured it."

"Now you're grasping at virtual straws, Abby."

"Nope, I'm looking for them. I didn't know this guy Nero, but no one deserves to have his killer get away with murder. It's my job and pleasure to put jerks away."

"That's not your job, lady, and you know it."

"Okay." Abby took a deep breath and recited in a monotone, "It's my job to gather convincing data so that – in conjunction with it and other evidence collected by designated officers of the law, and witness testimonies – killers can be tried by a jury of their peers, convicted in a court of law, and put away...with other jerks."

"You're right. It's easier to say, 'It's my job to put jerks away.'"

"So. I'm ready to get started. Do me a favor and grab me a couple of candy bars. I'm not stopping for dinner, and I wiped out my secret stash on the way to the scene."

"I'll do one better. I'll bring in real food. I want to go over some of this, too. And before you start protesting, I know it's not in my job description. Charlene and the kids are at the zoo today with their Kool Kinder Kids group. While you're doing your thing, I want to look closer at those pictures you snapped with your phone. Plus, whatever you have on that dandelion Winifred was so interested in."

"All the data in the world isn't as important as observing people at the scene of the crime, right? Isn't that what you always say?"

"Well," Arlie drawled, "Sometimes but not always."

"Do you think she had something to do with it?"

"Nope. I'm pretty sure she was emotionally involved with Nero, though. She was too quiet. Death never bothered her before. At least, not that I could see."

"She seemed mighty opinionated to me, like she'd already come to her own conclusions on who, why, and how but wasn't going to say anything. She was your teacher in cop school, right?"

"Yes, but that's because she was hurt in the line of duty. She had been a field agent for a long time. She was literally blasted out of her job by a homemade bomb. There wasn't much use for an operative who couldn't walk. Her brain was still as sharp as ever, so she changed occupations within the same agency."

"She's retired now, right?" Abby asked as she set Buzz on her charging stand and plugged her in. "As in, she wasn't there in any official capacity but just happened to be in the neighborhood?"

"Bingo. Nero was in Witness Protection. She shouldn't have known about it but did. I knew a bit about the old him…or who I think he was. He must have had some plastic surgery somewhere along the way."

She nodded. "So, which one do you want to analyze first: the photos on my phone or the data?"

"Share the photos on your monster monitor. Maybe something is more obvious when viewed really, *really* up close."

Abby tapped and swiped her phone a couple of times, and an image of Nero's wound popped into view on her sixty-five-inch ultra-high-definition screen.

"Damn," Arlie hissed. "Not what I thought. At least, not that I can verify with that shot."

"Don't tell me what you suspect, or you'll skew my analyses towards that. Now, go play somewhere else."

Abby shooed Arlie away toward her office and its desktop computer, away from all her finely calibrated equipment and laptop. "But don't forget, you said you're buying dinner."

Arlie rubbed his belly. "Sooner than later. I can't seem to get the aroma of pasta and sourdough garlic bread out of my head. I'm ordering in right away."

***

Forty minutes later

"You owe me," Abby growled.

49

Startled, Arlie spun around toward her uncharacteristically low voice. "Whoa. That doesn't happen very often."

"Me using my bossy voice or scaring you?" Abby chuckled as he composed himself. "I don't think I've ever seen you jump. I noticed the delivery guy pulling up on the security monitor and decided to head him off in the parking garage."

She stuck her nose in the large paper bag, inhaled deeply, and pulled away with a huge smile. "I paid this time. I guess I'll go gluten-free later. I'm not passing on this. What'd you get?"

"I told them I wanted two of whatever today's special was, plus double on the garlic bread. Too bad we can't have red wine with it."

"We'll have to forgo the candles, too," Abby joked as she brushed the sleeve of her smock across the counter, clearing folders aside to make way for the food. "Unless you want me to scrounge up some Bunsen burners."

"I'll save the Chianti and candles for Charlene. This is just sustenance. I guess I'm craving it because Nero was Italian. I knew if I didn't give in and get some, I wouldn't be able to concentrate on my work."

Abby pulled the foil and cardboard dishes out of the bag while Arlie got bottled water and paper towel placemats. *"Mangia!"*

"Here's to inspiration," Arlie replied, offering her a bottle. He took a big bite of the garlicky bread and frowned. "It smells good, but it doesn't taste as good as Nero's. Louie was right. The man's sourdough was sublime."

"Here's hoping it's good enough to inspire answers from all that information we collected," Abby said, saluting him with the toasted bread. She took a nibble. "Tastes great to me."

"It'll have to do. I think our days of eating Mount Spurr Sourdough are done. If you don't mind, I'll take mine to your desk. I'm going to go over as much data as I can in the next three hours." Arlie looked up at the clock on the wall. "Charlene and the Kinder Kids were going out for pizza after the zoo. If I time it right, we should all get home about the same time."

"Since when did you decide to work with me at the lab rather than review everything from your laptop at home?"

Arlie laughed. "That's easy. Since Louie moved next door. He's a great guy but loves to pop in and 'help' me."

"And by help you mean he distracts you?"

"Yup." Arlie set the bread on top of the container of pasta and grabbed a few napkins and the plastic fork. "Now, don't you do it, too."

"My mouth is only open for food unless I find something big, as in conclusive evidence."

"Back at ya. I won't keep my findings a secret, either."

***

Before Arlie started into his main course, he tapped notes into his phone, little ticklers he'd follow up on after he'd scanned the fields of data. Abby had already picked up on a few of them. Why was Winifred there, what was her interest in the dandelion, and how come there was a relative lack of mess from Nero's gut wound?

And why had he died with a smile?

No, that one was easy.

Nero knew his murderer and wasn't going to let the man see him suffer.

Or was it 'the woman' see him suffer?

Arlie shifted in his seat, uncomfortable with the thought.

Winifred couldn't be a part of this, could she?

Was she a spurned lover? Did she call him and Jess in because she thought they wouldn't suspect her?

"Ah, shut up and eat," he mumbled. "You're getting lightheaded and squirrelly. She couldn't be the murderer."

Or could she?

Chapter 7: Ice Cream Social: Pleasure and Pain

Three hours later

"Abby, it's time for me to split. Did you find anything on those gloves?"

"Of course, I found something."

"All right. I'll bite. *What* did you find on those gloves?"

"You mean, besides water?"

"Actually, I meant were you able to get any fingerprints or partials from the inside of them."

"Nothing conclusive, but I did find something unusual on the outside." Abby paused and waited for Arlie's scowl of impatience.

"Don't make me wait. I just got a text. Charlene and the kids are leaving the pizza place now. After all the bouncing around they did, they'll be ready for ice cream by the time they get home. She said if I make them wait too long, it'll be gone by the time I get there."

"Okay. There's dirt and chlorophyll on the gloves. No biggie since they were thrown on plants in the garden, but there's also yeast. As in, lots of it."

"What kind of yeast? The kind from an infection or had the murderer been making bread?"

"Making it or eating it."

"I didn't see any signs anyone had been in Nero's house much less the kitchen. His place was still locked up tight enough that I could have designed the security."

"Buzz came to the same conclusion," Abby said with pride. "If Nero was such a great baker, you might want to see if someone was trying to knock him out as competition."

Arlie shook his head. "No, not likely"

"Why not?" Abby asked, hands on hips, indignant.

"I said not likely, not absolutely not. Maybe the suspect was just a fan and couldn't find Nero's bread anywhere. Maybe he dropped by his house to try and get some in person. I know he only sells to wholesalers, but if this guy – or gal – didn't know that and had found him unwilling to sell to him…"

Arlie shrugged. "It could be the murder knew nothing about Nero being in Witness Protection but was an out of control, obsessed fan." He paused. "Or someone who wanted his sourdough starter to make his own bread."

"Now who's grasping at straws or creating them?" Abby teased.

Arlie shook his head. "Just thinking out loud. You said the yeast was on the outside of his glove or gloves. If he was a baker, it would be on his face, arms, hands, and under his fingernails, too – anywhere it could settle while mixing dough or kneading it. Would you see if your little boy-toy Manny took surface skin samples?"

Abby growled and started to protest but stopped when Arlie shook his head and laughed. "Sorry. Bad joke. If he didn't get any, grab some, please. Samples, that is. If there *was* some killer competition going on between bakers, there'll be yeast everywhere."

"Got it. Go have a double scoop cone for me. With sprinkles."

Arlie nodded. "Will do. That is, if Chip hasn't eaten all the cones already. It's a 'for sure' on the sprinkles, though. I put those up high enough, he couldn't get them." His levity dropped and sincerity stepped in. "Don't work too late. You have a family now, too."

"Yeah…ain't it great?"

"That it is."

***

As soon as Arlie was gone, Abby headed toward the morgue to collect the samples he had asked for.

"Hey, Miss Abby," a voice called out, startling her.

"Oh, hi, Henry. I didn't see you," she said, greeting the janitor with a smile.

"I got a call from the new guy, Manny. He said there was a mess he wanted cleaned up stat. I thought someone got sick or something. He just wanted the trash thrown out right away."

Henry shook his head and walked around his cart. "You know, I've been doing this job for nearly ten years without complaints. Then this guy comes in and messes up my whole routine, wantin' me to do a trash run at his end of the building first, not the last. And look at this? Isn't this the kind of stuff that's supposed to be sent south to the big labs?"

Abby looked into the bag Henry was holding open. It was filled with specimen trays, tubes, and vials. She took a pair of gloves out of her pocket, slipped them on, and picked out two small containers. 'Smiley' was written on both labels. "Is this the first time you've seen these thrown in the morgue's trash?"

"Yes, ma'am. I even told him I thought he was makin' a mistake. They weren't even put in a red hazmat bag first. He made a few derogatory remarks about my job level compared to his, that I shouldn't be worrying about what wasn't my business, so I didn't. Well, not much. At least, that he could tell. I was makin' my way up to you to ask about it. I know my job is just as important as anyone else's, but I didn't think I should tell him that. I don't think he's a very nice fella." Henry shook his head. "Nope, not nice at all."

"I'll get these boxed up and sent out like they should have been. Until we can catch him in the act, though, don't say anything to him or anyone else."

"Yes, Miss Abby. I'm sure he's the kind of person who'd find a way to blame me for everything." Henry tipped his Anchorage Pilots baseball cap. "I'd best be gettin' the rest of my job done. Have a good night now."

"You, too. Oh, and thanks."

Abby watched Henry walk down the hall, whistling an old country song as pushed his janitorial cart, his perky attitude as unmistakable as his off-kilter gait.

***

"Daddy's home, Daddy's home," the boys hollered, the seven-year-old brothers' excitement echoed by their toddler sister.

"Now we can eat ice cream, huh, Mom?" Chip asked.

Charlene reached up and tried to grab the cones out of the top cabinet.

"Here, let me help," Arlie said, giving her a quick peck on the cheek. "I think I pushed them a little too far back last time."

Charlene moved the half-gallon of ice cream out of his way from the counter onto the kitchen table. "I took this out a few minutes ago so it'd be easier to scoop out."

Arlie set his hand down where the ice cream had been and paled.

"What's wrong?" she asked.

"Wrong? Nothing." He rubbed his hands together, his mind racing. "I just realized something important, though. Don't worry. I'll fix the cones and sprinkles first. Work can come later. If you want to scoop, I'll get the sprinkles. Close your eyes, boys. I don't want you to see where I hid them."

"Ah, Dad," Chip whined.

Carlos elbowed him and their little sister giggled. "Daddy can't find them now 'cause Mommy hid them again."

"Got 'em," Arlie crowed.

"But...but," the kids stammered.

"And I moved them back again," Charlene said. "Never underestimate your parents, children. Just when you think you have them figured out, they surprise you."

Five minutes later, all the cones were assembled, and the gang was ready to indulge in their colorful desserts. Carlos took a big bite of his ice cream and yelped in pain. He handed the cone to Chip. "Here, you can have it. I'm not hungry anymore."

"Are you sure it's not just brain freeze?" Arlie asked.

Carlos shrugged, then shook his head, trying not to cry. His frown of agony betrayed him, though.

Charlene turned on the tap and got him a cup of warm water. "This should help."

He sipped some, then ran outside and spat it out.

"Nope. I'd say someone has a cavity and needs to see the dentist," Arlie said.

"Not me," Chip mumbled through one hand clasped over his mouth, the other precariously holding two cones.

"Good detective work, Dad," Charlene said. She took the second cone from Chip and looked for a place to put it. She set an empty coffee cup on a paper plate and balanced the cone in it.

"Look at that, kids. That's a prime example of Engineering 101. Your mom saw a problem and created a solution. She devised a support system that won't smash the sprinkles on the ice cream, and any dribbles will be caught by the disposable dish beneath it."

"It's just a cup and a paper plate," Chip scoffed.

"Yes, but everyday products used in new and novel ways is what makes an average person a genius or an engineer..." Arlie squatted next to his young daughter, glanced at the counter where he'd felt the cold spot, and grinned. "Or a detective."

"I'll call Doc Puller first thing in the morning," Charlene said. "Why don't you lie down on the couch, Carlos. The pain will subside in a few minutes. Both cold and sweet foods can make even the smallest cavity hurt."

"Speaking of detective work," Arlie said, "if our ice cream social is over, I have some data to go over. This time, working from home provided the inspiration I needed. If Buzz did her job right, she may have collected some essential information."

"Go ahead. I'll let Chip eat the last of the ice cream out of the carton if he helps me clean up."

Chip belched, then quickly said, "Excuse me!" He groaned softly. "I'll help, but I don't need any more ice cream for a while. I guess two and a half cones is my limit."

"Two and a half?" Charlene asked. "I knew you finished the one Carlos had, but where'd you get the other half?"

He looked to his little sister, licking the remains of her chocolate ice cream from the hem of her blouse. "She was going kind of slow, so I helped her out. No more for me for a long, long time."

***

Arlie made a quick phone call from the den. "Hey, Abby. I think when you sent me Buzz's file, you missed a few categories. Did you upload all of them?"

"No, not yet. I got distracted with a call from the custodian. It seems like Manny was trying to bury – or rather, trash – a few of the samples he was supposed to send out. I almost got it taken care of. After I'm done sealing this box for shipment, I'll send the rest of the data. That should only take a minute or five."

"Okay. I have one more daddy duty, then it's back to work. I don't know how moms do it, but I'm glad they do."

"Hey, dads can multitask, too," Abby said. "I know mine did. Hey, gotta jet to catch the courier. See ya."

Arlie came back out and read the kids their bedtime stories.

Despite the protests, he finished for the evening, insisting three was enough for anyone. He tucked in the boys then took Harlie Jae to her room and kissed her goodnight.

"Goodnight, kids," he called out from the hall.

"Goodnight, Dad," they chorused, then snuggled down.

Sweet ice cream dreams, everyone.

***

Arlie plopped down on the living room couch and relaxed into it with a loud sigh.

"Rough day?" Charlene asked, coming in to sit down beside him.

"Not really, at least for me. Louie and Jess lost their caterer, though."

Arlie watched his wife's eyebrow rise and clarified. "Lost as in…well, you know."

"Oh."

He shrugged and grimaced. "Yeah. Winifred and Jess are involved in solving this, too."

Charlene inhaled deeply as realization hit. "So, if both you and Jess are working on this, then Louie wants to 'help' too, right?"

Arlie nodded then chuckled. "You know, he really does contribute at times. It's just I'm afraid he's going to get hurt or jeopardize his own hiding in plain sight status by hanging around bad guys. Eventually, someone's going to notice his speech or mannerisms. Whether he's brunette or redhead, brown-eyed or blue, using the name Lucky or Louie – he's one of a kind. And hard to miss."

Carlos sneaked out of bed, hoping Chip was asleep. His first mother had rubbed some sort of magic potion on his teeth when they hurt before. Maybe Mom had some, too.

"What are they talkin' about, Carlos?" Chip whispered.

Carlos closed the door completely and shooed his brother back to bed. "Mostly grown-up stuff, but a little about Louie, too. When he was my 'almost brother' before I met you and Mom and Dad, he had black hair and brown eyes. They're talking about that. He looked kinda weird." Carlos shrugged. "And he wasn't very nice to me, either."

Chip shook his head. "But he's so nice now. What happened? Did an alien take over his body or something?"

"Nah. He told me he had to pretend he was someone else to impress people. I don't think he liked it, either. He was never happy."

"Yeah, well, Uncle Louie's happy most of the time now. I mean, I know he's really happy being a dad and uncle and having Jess around. I guess being a brother didn't work for him like it does for you and me. I hope you don't change and want to be my uncle instead of my brother. I like it fine just the way we are."

"Yeah, me, too," Carlos said, content again. "Come on, let's go to sleep. My tooth doesn't hurt so bad anymore."

***

"If you don't mind, I want to get back to this," Arlie said, nodding to his laptop. "It shouldn't take too long."

"Don't worry about me. I have a good book to read." Charlene picked up her paperback, the travel version of LOST she carried with her everywhere. "I always have this with me now."

She looked inside the front cover and the penned-in dates. "One, two, three, four. This is the fifth time I've read it. There's a new one coming out in six months. Time to reread the whole series."

"Reread them all again," he corrected. "Yes, I read that one when I lived in Fairbanks."

"That's right. Your neighbor gave you this one to read. Whatever happened to her? Dani, was it?"

Arlie grinned and shook his head. "I'm not sure. She literally disappeared. Remember Billy Burke, the detective who visited from North Carolina with his son Mac a while back?"

"Who could forget them? That little Mac was such a sweetheart. Oh, how he loved calling me Mom…"

"Yeah," Arlie said, breaking into her reverie, "Well, Billy and I were talking about unsolved mysteries once. I brought up Dani. His face paled so much, I thought he was going to puke!"

"What?"

Arlie laughed. "Talk about a 'Gotcha!' I knew he knew something. 'Do me a favor,' he said. 'Don't investigate. Trust me. She's safe. Don't ask me how I know but trust me. She and Leah are fine.' And that was that."

"Wait. What? You just let it drop?" Charlene asked.

"Yup. I don't know if you want to call it professional courtesy, or maybe it's just a guy thing. You know, respecting each other's requests." He shrugged.

"But…but…"

"But nothing. I'm sure he's right. She's fine. I never met her daughter, Leah, but if she's half as sharp and tough as Dani, I'm positive both are doing well wherever they are."

"Where could they be that you can't find them?"

"Totally off everyone's radar. Billy knows, but it's not much of a secret if it's shared. I can respect that."

"You're right," Charlene said as she stood up. "Men really are different from women. It's more than plumbing, too. Let me know if you need anything." She bent to kiss him. "Goodnight for now."

Arlie picked up his laptop and pulled back the recliner lever. "Now, what do we have here…"

After scrolling through the files Abby had uploaded to the cloud, he found what he was looking for: temperature readings. He opened the photo folder on his phone, zoomed in on the area, and overlaid the coordinates grid.

"Yup, a drop in temperature right where that dandelion was. Or is. What did you find there, Winifred?" he mused, comparing the soil temperatures and the image of the bent-but-not-broken weed.

"To be continued in the morning," Arlie said, closing the laptop. "I can't do anything else tonight. I think I'll go read over Charlene's shoulder for a bit." He purred in contentment. "Or we can do a little romancing of our own."

***

The next morning

    Knock, knock.

Arlie started to rise from the recliner, then saw it was Louie. Charlene was already at her foster brother's elbow, trying to lead him away.

"I told you he was working and didn't want to be disturbed, Louie," she said.

"Yeah, but it's just me, and I'm his helper. I can help him solve it, I know I can."

Jess put one hand on his fiancé's shoulder, ready to assist Charlene. "There, the girls are both penned in and stacking blocks," he told her. "Come on, Louie. Let Arlie work alone until he asks for help. Besides, I think LuLu and Harlie Jae are learning to cooperate. I want to get videos of their first joint venture."

"They're working together as a team? Hey, just like their dads – like Arlie, you, and me."

Arlie looked up and saw Louie was wearing the Chugiak Chinooks baseball cap Winifred had given him at the crime scene. He talked into the brim, "Why don't we share info on this one, Winifred? Like the man said, there's a better chance of solving a crime with teamwork."

"Are you okay, Arlie?" Louie asked. "It's me, not Winifred. Can't you tell the difference?" He paused and chuckled. "I'm prettier."

Suddenly, a loud air horn blast came out of the phone in Louie's shirt pocket.

"Dang it, Winifred!" he shouted. "Stop it! You're acting like a child."

"Me?" she hollered through the speakerphone. "You're the one who should grow a pair. You can't even pony up a quarter for a proper cuss word. Dang it?"

"Hey," Jess interjected. "He has a pair and a very nice pair at that."

Winifred sputtered in response, "Too… too much information."

"Well, you started it," Louie argued. "And Jess and I are parents now. We gotta keep it clean because we never know when a kid's gonna pop in."

"Yeah, huh?" Chip crowed. "Hey, Dad. Can I have tablet time? Mom said I did a good job cleanin' up, the girls are playin' with their blocks and that's boring, and Carlos is lying down with a washcloth on his toothache and doesn't want to do nothin'. I'm bored."

Arlie moved into the middle of the group, shook his head, and waved his hands in the air, trying to weave chaos into order. "So much for being alone to get work done. Chip, yes, you can have tablet time if it's okay with your mom. Louie, right now, I'm working on preliminaries. I don't want to get distracted with 'who is' and 'what ifs' on my first review of the data I have. Jess, thanks for dropping by."

"See, I told you we could help him," Louie said.

"Not what I meant," Arlie said. "Jess, thanks for coming by to keep Louie busy. I have more than enough helpers volunteering."

Jess noticed the dot of the letter 'i' of the word Chinook on Louie's hat glimmered. He walked in front of it. "Hey, Winnie. How do you like the See-Hawks cap Arlie gave me?" He tipped it toward her but didn't take it off. "It's a lot like the one you gifted Louie, but maybe – no, probably – better."

Arlie stepped next to him and grinned into the tiny optical device. "Come on, Winifred. Why were you so fascinated with that dandelion? You can tell me." He turned around to the group. "Everyone out. Winifred and I have work to do."

Jess and Charlene shooed everyone out of the room. Or tried to.

"She's still on my phone," Louie said. "You can talk to her on it, but that means I have to stay…"

Click.

"She hung up, Louie," Arlie said. "I'll call her back on mine."

One-eyed, one-horned, flying purple people eater…

"And there she is."

Arlie answered Winifred's personalized ringtone with a quick, "Hold on a sec," then turned to the others. "Goodbye, Louie. You know I'll ask for your input when I'm ready. For now, I need to gather my thoughts while the evidence is fresh in my mind. Oh, and make sure you get a video of the girls building bridges or skyscrapers or whatever together. I'm sure they'll be helping the boys build birdhouses before you know it."

"Will do," Jess said, leading Louie away.

"Thanks for holding, Winifred. You know how Louie is. So, before we get interrupted again, what's the deal with the dandelion?"

"It has nothing to do with the case," she said coolly.

The lack of snippy comeback or irritation at being asked again indicated to Arlie that the yellow-flowered weed *was* important.

Winifred was hiding something. Rather than pursue the subject, he decided to let her lead the discussion. She was the one who had called him to the scene. How come she was there?

"So, while I'm thinking about it, why did you call both Jess *and* me? Couldn't make up your mind whether this was a local or federal case?"

"The short and easy answer is because you're both discreet. Also, between the two of you, you have access to more information than I could ever have by calling in favors."

"Which is the only way you'd get any info since you're no longer employed by any agency. I understand, Winifred. Retirement must be frustrating, but how did you find out about the murder in the first place?"

"You know, I'm pretty good at reading voices, too, Arlie. You're dying to ask me something else. Go ahead. Spit it out."

"I just did. How. Did. You. Know. About. It?"

"That's not important," Winifred said, her voice suddenly curt and icy.

Arlie waited for her to say more. She needed him and that was his trump card. He put the phone on speaker, set it down, and grabbed his laptop, waiting for her to answer. He could multitask while she decided whether to work with him or be the stubbornest old lady in the state.

"What did you find with your little spy drone?"

"I'm not answering any of your questions until you answer mine," Arlie said, hoping she could hear the grin in his voice. Playing hardball with a former teacher truly was sweet.

Winifred took a deep breath and sighed in frustration. "I went there because he didn't answer my phone call, okay?"

"Now was that so hard?" Arlie teased. "As to your question, I'm reviewing the data Buzz collected right now. So far, it's just a series of numbers and a long list of chemicals. Abby should have more data soon. She assisted in the autopsy. I'd say she probably collected enough samples to keep the lab boys and girls busy for a while."

"Well, that was a gracious way of saying nothing," Winifred chided.

"Thank you."

"It wasn't a compliment."

Arlie sighed. "You know, you're just as bad as Louie. Leave me alone for a while, would you? Let me sort this puzzle, or at least get an idea of what picture is on it. I'd ask what your interest is – or was – in Nero, but that can come later. I'll let you have your little secret for now. If I don't need to know, I won't ask."

"You don't need to know," Winifred said, her voice chilly again.

"Not for now, I don't. So, say goodbye and let me get my job done. Why don't you go do whatever it is little old, retired detective spy teachers do when they're bored? Quit bothering active-duty personnel while they work."

"This little old lady never did get bored with her work. And for the record, I didn't give up my job – it was taken from me."

"Yeah, I guess it was. Sorry about that, Winifred. I'll call if I need help. Right now, everyone's out of my face, and I have some quiet time to think. Let me do that, will you?"

"Sure."

Click.

Arlie opened the file with the temperature readings and superimposed it over a recent image of the yard.

Yup. Just what he suspected.

The slightly bent but not broken dandelion was fifteen degrees cooler than the surrounding ground. Why? It seemed too simple to be true.

Nero's body still had residual heat left because of his vast amount of body-fat insulation. Had the murderer stayed to watch him die or left after mortally wounding him? Was he still in the state?

So many questions. If Nero's smile had been as unsettling to his attacker as it was to everyone else, the murderer – or murderess – hadn't stayed around.

Why would Nero, a man in Witness Protection – who had already been relocated three times after ratting on his former assassin buddies – not have a security system in place?

Especially if he was involved with a cyber-queen like Winifred…

And there he had it.

Winifred had been spying on Nero. When his video feed disappeared, she came by to find out why.

Now he had to find out who did it…

And how.

CHAPTER 8: HOW TO MIX WORK
AND PLEASURE

Palmer-Wasilla Highway
Late the next morning

"Yesterday almost too easy. Of course, practice – and much experience – make perfect." Yakov chuckled then roared with laughter. "Oh, that is right. Practice *is* experience!"

Yakov drove down the highway, ignoring the speed limit in his newly acquired silver Mercedes sedan. Sunlight bounced off the hood, brightening his already glorious mood. "Practice, practice, practice. Who says you cannot mix work and pleasure?"

His face fell as he remembered the kiss he'd stolen from his secret crush. He'd waited so long to be close to Sonny – Nero, as he chose to be called in his new life. Yakov cranked up the heavy metal music on the radio, determined to drown out his misgivings and mixed emotions.

"I not only stole your heartbeat but maybe now your secret life as bread maker." He shouted over the tunes, "Now people will praise *my* baking skills. I, too, can have new life here in land of Northern Lights and sled dogs. I have your baking notes and recipes. I will hire high dollar promoter and soon, my breads will be greatest trend since online porn! I will have local peoples do work, keep them in line by paying big bucks or maybe just heavy hand and big stick. Then I fly to Thailand, the land of many perverted pleasures. Then I will be legitimate millionaire!"

Whoop! Whoop!

"*Diermo!* What now?" He glanced over at his radar detector and saw the warning light flashing. "Damned music too loud."

Whoop! Bleep! Bleep! Wang! Wang! Wang!

Yakov looked in the rearview mirror. The lights atop the Alaska State Trooper's vehicle were now in strobe mode, the headlights flashing like fireworks exploding. The siren had changed from its 'get-your-attention whoop-whoop' warning and was now blasting discordant tones at mixed volume levels. Too late to say he hadn't seen the cop. "Time to pull over and play dumb."

***

Trooper Adams called into his dispatcher. "As soon as I'm done here, I'm clocking out for the day. Abigail's not due for a week, but she said she had a backache. This might be the real deal, and she's already in labor. I don't want to miss even a minute of it. If this one is anything like the first two, she'd better not so much as sneeze. That kid will come out whether the midwife's there or not."

The trooper kept his eye on the radar gun as he spoke. "Shoot. Looks like I caught a fast one. I gotta pull this guy over, Gladys. FYI, my chest camera is still on the fritz. The dash mount unit's working, though. I'll make sure I'm lined up with it, so at least everything done is recorded. For some reason, this doesn't seem to be my day. At least, at work,"

"It might not be your day for electronics, Adams, but as long as you get home safely, it's all good. And remind Abigail that I'm still pulling for another girl."

73

"Yeah, yeah, yeah," the tired trooper said. "And if it is, I'm pretty sure we'll put Gladys in there somewhere as one of her middle names. It still wouldn't bother me if we had a son. Eventually, I'd like to be able to leave the toilet seat up."

"You can do that now."

"Let me clarify, leave it up without being hollered at. Okay, I'm pulling over a late-model silver Mercedes. Damn! No plates, either. This doesn't look good."

"Whatever you do, don't agitate him. Let him off with a warning and stick one of those little trackers Arlie gave you on the back end. Someone else can deal with him if he's dirty. You have a wife and kids…"

"I know, I know. I'm getting out now."

"Be safe," Gladys said, knowing he was already out and had shut the door. She tapped on her computer and brought up his dash cam image. "Damn! Mud-splattered ass end. Put it somewhere else. Just don't forget the tracker, don't forget the tracker," she mumbled as a soft-spoken mantra. "This doesn't look good."

***

"Is there a problem?" Yakov asked in his best American accent.

"Step out of the car for a moment, sir," Adams said. He stepped back to give the man room to get out but also to get a better view of the inside of the vehicle. No weapons in sight. Now was not the time to make a comment about the radar detector light flashing on the dash.

"Oh, sorry, but I cannot," Yakov said, his door half-opened. He patted his left knee. "I just have surgery. Muscle get tight on me. I did not notice my speed go faster. Was I happen to go over limit when rubbing knee?"

"Yes, according to my radar, you were going ninety miles an hour. That's a felony rate in this state, sir."

"Oh, I very sorry, officer. Can you let me off with warning? I promise to put car on cruise control for rest of way home. I no want happen again. I almost home now. I no drive again. I ask daughter to take me to next week doctor appointment. And I was today thinking I do so well..." Yakov sighed and shook his head in feigned self-admonishment.

Trooper Adams bit back his bile at the obvious lie. He probably didn't have knee surgery much less a daughter. Pure fabrication. The man's accent and piss-poor grammar were probably real, though. If this guy wasn't Russian, he was at least Eastern European. He wasn't in the mood to challenge him, though. With Abigail in labor, he didn't want to start any flammable confrontations.

Adams glanced at the dealer's maintenance sticker on the inside of the car door, then down at the serial number plate. The first digit was one, then the next four characters were his two daughter's initials. The last six digits were his wife's birthdate. "Looks like you're due for an oil change, sir. I'll tell you what. You go home and ice that knee. And stay away from driving until you get the doctor's release. If you promise to do that, I'll let you off with a verbal warning."

"Sound good for me, officer," Yakov said, doing his best to keep the sneer out of his voice.

The trooper held onto the roof frame as he shut the door. With his thumb, he wiped away accumulated grit, cleaning off a spot for the disguised chip. Then he patted the roof in farewell, attaching Arlie's tracker at the same time. If the man truly was a crook and not just a scofflaw speeder, now they'd find him, with or without a license plate.

Yakov started the engine and put the car in gear. He stuck his hand out the window, desperately wanting to flip off the trooper. Instead, all fingers stayed together, and he waved goodbye, fighting the urge to peel out and fling back gravel. "It is your lucky day, cop," he said under his breath. "Very lucky."

***

Trooper Adams watched as the man put his hand out the window to wave farewell. The fist clenched then opened out, as if ready for a karate chop. Yes, this guy was evil. A chill ran up his spine. He felt as if he'd just dodged a bullet. "Must be my lucky day."

"Are you okay?" Gladys called over the radio at his shoulder.

He turned toward his cruiser and waved at her via its dash cam. "Yeah, I am. But before I forget it, run this serial number. I didn't get all the middle digits, but it's a late model C Class Mercedes. See if it was stolen."

"Did you bug it?"

"What? Do you think I'd let someone off that easy without a way to check up on him? He's so rotten, I'm surprised flies weren't buzzing around him. I'm done for today, though. I'm going home to help the midwife bring another Adams into the world."

"You do that. I'll give Arlie a heads up on the tracker. He'll see it but won't know who activated it or why. Anything you want me to add other than the man was speeding and didn't have plates?"

"Yeah. Tell him the man was a lousy liar from Eastern Europe who sounded like he learned English from Cookie Monster on Sesame Street. He was driving what may have been a stolen car. Give him that partial VIN. He can probably fill in the missing characters better than a computer."

"Will do."

***

"That almost too easy, too." Yakov looked into his rearview mirror to make sure he wasn't being followed. "Now to find bakery with right kind of oven – Nero's notes say it very important. It not good plan to take over brick oven at his home. Too suspicious. Palmer or Wasilla close enough. Delivery trucks and planes run all day and night, da? Who knows? Yakov bread maybe become world famous!"

Yakov nodded as he fantasized, proud of his sneaky way of 'retiring.' Taking over someone else's life this way, without ratting on his friends or getting help from 'goodfellas' was clever. He was an independent agent – a lone wolf – and proud of it.

A bright light on the dash caught his attention. The radar-buster device flashed the numeral eighty-five. "Damn." He slowed down to sixty-five, set the cruise control, and kept his eyes forward as he passed a Wasilla policeman getting back in his vehicle. Don't look guilty, don't look guilty…

Vroom!

A cherry-red Corvette convertible sped past Yakov in the outside lane, going at least a hundred miles per hour.

"Go get him, pig," Yakov laughed. He looked into his rearview mirror and watched the cop scramble to get into his cruiser. "Da. Everything almost too easy here."

***

Yakov straight-arm pushed the door open at the first bakery he had found on his phone. "What kind of oven you have here?" he asked loudly, announcing his arrival to what looked like an empty store.

"Good afternoon, sir," a gray-haired woman said, walking in from the food prep area behind her. She wiped flour from her hands on the bar towel she kept by the cash register and gave him her full attention. "We have a brick oven which stays on eleven months a year."

"Why only eleven?" Yakov asked. Swirls of white, yellow, and brown caught his eye and he looked down two feet. An artistic array of pastries in the display case in front of him not only looked good, but their smell made him hungry.

"We take a three-week vacation every year," she said with a broad grin. "Hawaii's just a short plane ride away from Alaska."

"That still leave one week."

"That's about how long it takes us to get back up to speed. Or rather, to temperature. We make sure we have enough of the right kind of wood for the oven and that it's seasoned, not damp. Reactivating enough starter for all the dough we'll need for the first run takes a week, too. While that's working, we go through all the racks and pans, replace what's needed, order supplies, create the specials calendar, check in with our distributors to see if they want to increase or decrease their usual orders, and finally, set up a few promotions, so we can get more customers."

"Sounds like much work. I thought you just mix dough and cook bread."

The woman chuckled. "Yeah, that's how it was when my husband baked just for family, friends, and co-workers. Back then, he was working full time in Anchorage and only baked for special events. Eventually, his friends talked him into to starting a full-time bakery. Who knew running a business would be so much work?"

"You want to sell business and retire maybe?" Yakov asked, the smell of cinnamon and apples rekindling his greed and bringing a smile to his face.

She shook her head. "Not yet. Now, ask me in about two months when the bills are due, and my employees call in sick when I know they're really just hungover." The woman nodded, her eyes glazed over as she recalled the harried hours that turned into sleepless days of baking, wrapping, and delivering for her lazy, inconsiderate crew. "Yeah, in two months, I might just sell this place real cheap."

"Okay. I come back later maybe. For now, fill box with some of everything sweet and make bag of different kinds of bread. I might be hungry later."

Donna grabbed a sheet of cardboard and quickly flipped it open into a flat box. She was assembling an assortment of pastries when Yakov interrupted her.

"Hey, you. Give me one of those now. For road."

She took a fresh waxed tissue and wrapped it around the biggest apple fritter on the shelf. "Here you go. For the road and on the house. Let me get a bag for the breads. Do you want them sliced?"

Yakov scowled as he tried to figure out what she meant.

"For sandwiches or toast. It's your choice. No extra charge. It will take a minute to get six loaves done, though."

"No. I have knife. I cut good." He smiled broadly. "Very good."

Donna looked down as she rang up his purchase. Before she could tell him the total, he had grabbed the bread and pastries and was pushing his way out the door. Two one-hundred-dollar bills were on the counter, the wadded-up wax tissue from his fritter sitting on top of them.

"Thanks," she said softly to the empty air behind him. "Best tip I've ever had."

Yakov set the box of sweets and sack of bread on the seat beside him. Without turning around, he stomped on the gas and backed out of the parking lot, just missing the family in the minivan pulling in.

"Watch it!" the driver screamed.

"Aw-full!" the woman beside her yelled.

Yakov ignored them as he sped onto the access road, cutting off a delivery truck, causing the man to swerve into the next lane.

"Pick up deli meat, cheese, olive oil, and stay low for few days," he said, ignoring the chaos around him. "I come out of hotel when food and cops are gone."

***

"Watch it!" Charlene screamed at the man backing out of his parking spot at rocket speed and without looking around.

"Aw-full!" Rita hissed, wishing that just this once she could say the real word. Louie was right, though. Substituting a biological synonym might work for a while, but the children would soon learn what rectum meant. 'Aw-full' wasn't the best substitute but really did describe the driver's behavior.

"I'm sorry I talked you into stopping here," Rita said. "If Louie wasn't so fussy about his darned apple fritters, we could have picked up some with the rest of the groceries."

"Yes, but you're right. A stack of fritters for his birthday really is the perfect gift. Well, perfect except for the fact that they'll be gone so fast. I was going to bake a cake for him but," Charlene's eyes brightened, the terror of the near miss in the parking lot forgotten.

She clicked the seatbelt button. "Instead, I called ahead and reserved a carrot cake. Losing the last ten pounds of baby weight is going to take a few weeks longer. I just can't resist…"

"Mom, are we getting that carrot cake you like so much?" Carlos asked.

"Yeah, huh?" Chip added. "'Cause if we are, that can be our vegetable for dinner tonight."

"Yes and no," Charlene said. "Yes, we're getting the cake. And no, it's not a substitute for your other vegetables. But don't worry. Rita and I are putting together a special Chinese food dinner."

"All by yourselves?" Chip asked.

"Yes and no."

"Mom," Carlos asked with dramatic exasperation. "Either you are or you aren't. Everything doesn't have to be a yes or no answer, you know."

"You sound just like Chip when you talk like that, Carlos. Okay. Yes, Rita and I are cooking all by ourselves. But the whole dinner won't be cooked by us. It's a themed potluck."

"Okay," Carlos said in defeat, then whispered to Chip, "Whatever that is."

"Carlos, a potluck is like a potlatch," Charlene said. "Remember when we had one for Tina's sister at the hospital?"

Both boys bounced up and down in place, excited but kept in place by their seatbelts. "Is Wanda coming, too? Maybe she and Tina can show us a few new basketball tricks," Chip said.

"Or we can have a game. Guys against the gals. Mom, Tina, Rita, and Wanda against us guys," Carlos added.

"Before you get too wound up, I'm going to go in and get our goodies. Rita, do you mind staying in the car? I hate to wake the girls."

Rita turned back and saw both her daughter and Charlene's were fast asleep. "No problem. I'm sure glad they keep to the same schedule. It makes life a lot easier."

"Napping is boring," Chip groaned. "I'll be glad when they're older and can play with us."

"Hey, be glad you got me," Carlos said. "Talk about boring. Before I was your brother, I was really bored."

"Yeah, you're right. I like having a bigger family. Even if LuLu isn't our sister, her dad's our uncle and lives next door."

Chip noticed his mother was halfway out of the car. "Hey, Mom. Would you get us a cookie? You can ask for one for Harlie Jae and LuLu, too. Carlos and I will help the girls eat them when they wake up."

"I'm sure you will. Yes, I'll ask for four cookies." Charlene looked at Rita. Her friend's mouth was open, ready to ask a question. "And I'll get one for you and me, too. It's a long time until supper."

Charlene saw Donna standing in the doorway of the bakery, frowning as she looked down the highway after her last patron. "And here I thought he was a good man because he gave me a big tip. I was sure he was going to hit you when he backed up."

"Yeah, me too. We're all okay. The boys didn't pay much attention to it. At least, it didn't distract them from asking for a cookie."

Donna walked in with her, then got busy behind the counter. She set out a paper bag and put two tissue-wrapped peanut butter cookies into it. "These aren't as messy as the snickerdoodles. Louie's fritters are ready to go, and it'll take only a minute to box up your cake. It's in the refrigerator."

"Before you go back, can you put in a couple little sugar cookies for the girls? Oh, and two chocolate chocolate-chip cookies, too? Those are for Rita and me. Our big guys will have to get their own."

"Tsk-tsk," Donna teased.

"If we got their treats now, they wouldn't make it home!"

"I never tire of hearing that." Donna paused. "I guess I'll have to

83

enjoy these moments now. I think Paul and I are going to retire."

"What?" Charlene yelped. She calmed down and asked, "Why would you want to do that?"

"This bakery is a lot of work. Getting up at oh-my-God-thirty to get fires stoked and breads rising, the cost of supplies either skyrocketing or the products aren't available at all. Dealing with unreliable employees, customers complaining about not enough selection or price increases… It goes on and on." Donna shook her head. "Sorry. It's not your problem. I'll be right back with the cake."

When she returned, Charlene reached out. "Hey, I wouldn't trade places with a small business owner right now or ever. It has to be tough."

"Well, sometimes it is. Actually, most times it is, but the tradeoff is usually worth it. We have a lot of freedom we wouldn't have if we were working for someone else. Paul and I had talked about retiring before but wanted to wait until one of our kids got the baking bug. We wanted one of them to step in and take over. It doesn't look like that's going to happen and well…" Donna huffed. "That man who almost backed into you expressed interest in buying us out. I don't know if he was serious or not. He was driving a nice car, and I think he's Russian, so I guess he might have the money for a big purchase like this."

"And if he's Russian and has a big family, they can help him keep it going. Don't be in a rush, Donna. Put up a poll on a few social media sites. Ask if folks think you should close the bakery or not. That'll bring them through these doors in a hurry. Everyone loves your breads and sweets. I know as soon as Louie found out he didn't have to go to Anchorage for apple fritters, you got a number one fan."

Donna giggled. "I know. I make sure I have some in the freezer just in case we run out up front. He told me once he wished I was his mother." She sighed and shook her head. "Such a sweet man."

"Yes, he is. Now, how much do I owe you for all this?"

Quickly keying most of the products into the cash register, Donna popped off a number.

"Don't forget to add in the cookies," Charlene said.

"Nah. Those are courtesy cookies. Even if I didn't use them as a promotional write-off on my taxes, that Russian gave me a big tip. Since I'm the only one working up front, it's all mine. It's a good day. Give Louie a hug and tell him it's from his other mother."

Charlene set the bag of cookies on top of the cake and was trying to figure out how to get the box of fritters, too, when Donna picked them up.

"Let me take a quick look at the kids. I haven't seen them in a month, at least."

When Rita saw the women laden with goodies approach, she got out of the car and opened the back. "Ah, it's going to be a sweet-smelling ride home."

"And sweet tasting, too," Chip said.

"No eating in the car," Rita announced.

"Ah, man," the boys groaned.

"Hey, we have to suffer, too," Charlene said. "Besides, when you get home, you can have a big glass of milk with your cookie. Not exactly the healthiest late morning snack ever, but it'll give you extra energy until this afternoon's surprise."

She took the box from Donna and added it to the other bags and boxes of food from the grocery store. "Thanks!"

"See you next time. Be careful out there. Crazy drivers are everywhere."

Once Charlene was buckled up and ready to go, Carlos asked, "Hey, Mom. What's this afternoon's surprise?"

"Yeah, huh?" Chip and Rita echoed.

Charlene put her hand up to shield her answer so only Rita could hear. She mouthed, 'No idea.'

Rita turned around and told the boys, "A surprise means you don't find out right away. Now sit back and see if you can think up new lyrics for happy birthday. Maybe 'Happy birthday to Lou' or something like that."

"Yeah, yeah," Carlos said. "But we'd better be quiet. We don't want to wake the girls or Mom won't give us the cookies and milk right away."

"Yeah, huh," Chip groaned. "She always has to take care of Harlie Jae first."

"And if you were the babies and she was the big sister, that's how I'd treat her, too. Now, knock it off, and let's get home."

Chip got excited and waved his hand in the air, trying to get Mom's attention. "How about 'Happy Birthday to Lou, you live in a zoo, you look like a monkey…"

"And eat like one, too," Carlos added.

"Sounds like a good start," Charlene said. "Keep it going but not too loud or you *will* have to wait for your snack."

CHAPTER 9: THE BIG TIPPER
OR THE BIG GYPPER

"Hey, Arlie. This is Gladys, your friendly Mat-Su Trooper dispatcher. Did you notice a new twinkle in your galaxy?"

"Don't you mean on my Galaxy? Yes, I did. So, that was you brightening up the southern regions of Wasilla?"

"Not directly. Andy Adams did the deed. His body cam was broken, but I got a good view of the stinker. Andy stopped him for speeding, but the car didn't have plates, either. I know it's not an excuse, but Mrs. Andy is going to pop out number three any minute now. I kinda pushed him – as in strongly suggested – he let the guy go with a warning and a tracker. He gave me a partial serial number for you, too. Oops! Hold, please."

Arlie heard Gladys put her cell phone on the table and answer an incoming call. He pulled over and waited for her to return, scanning the text messages he had received but not read while driving. "And there it is…"

Gladys had texted Arlie the make, model, and partial serial number a few minutes earlier. He quickly opened one of his custom apps, typed in the letters and numerals she had provided, and came up with a stolen vehicle report. "Well, well. Mister Green will be glad to hear his car hasn't left the state. Hopefully, it's still in good shape."

He opened the tracking app and selected an aqua blue hue for this tracker, making it easier to spot it in the splattered array of dots that represented the nearly two dozen vehicles he was monitoring.

"Sorry 'bout that," Gladys said, coming back on the line. "My day job has to come first. Being second-string Team Arlie means waiting on hold sometimes. Now, where were we before we were so rudely interrupted…"

"Serial number. Yes, I found the partial VIN you texted me," Arlie said. "I figured it out and found the car. I'm watching it now. Yup, it was stolen. I'll call it in. Andy's a sharp guy with great instincts. I guess it's a good thing he chose the Troopers over APD. It's nice to have eyes all over the state."

"Now, if you just had someone in the F.B.I. or U.S. Marshalls," Gladys mused, then giggled. "No, don't tell me. You already have."

"Okay. I won't tell you. Why did Andy pull him over to begin with? Just speeding?"

"It had to be mighty fast, or he suspected something else was fishy. Otherwise, he wouldn't have bothered. Once he stopped him, the guy was so full of crappy lies, he reeked. Andy also said it sounded as if English was the guy's second language – that he was probably from Russia or Eastern Europe. Since you have eyes on him now, I'm curious. Where did he take off to?"

Arlie expanded his view, then zoomed in. "Dang."

"Excuse me?"

Arlie groaned and put the phone in the holder on the dash. He watched as the aqua icon seemed to bounce off the pink one that represented Charlene, then pulled away. "He went to Wasilla."

"Yeah…" she prompted. "Since he was heading north on the

Glenn, it was either there or Palmer. What's the problem?"

Arlie right-clicked an option and viewed the recent history of the icons. "Double dang! He nearly crashed into my wife! I gotta scoot and check this out. Next time you talk to Andy, tell him I said you two make a good team. When that broken leg heals completely, you might want to see about teaming up with him."

"Teaming up again," Gladys said. "We went through the academy together. I became his best friend after I introduced him to my roommate."

"Let me guess. The present Mrs. Adams."

"The one and only. We can all chat about that another day. Time for both of us to get back to work."

"Ten-four," he said and ended the call.

Arlie got back on the highway, resisting the urge to bring out his magnetic mount emergency lights and signal his presence, clearing a path so he could race to his family unimpeded. Charlene wasn't in danger that he could see. "Keep a low profile, Arlie. It's easier to figure out what Mr. X is up to by laying low. X? No, that was last week's mystery man. I'm up to Mr. Y."

He bumped the cruise control up five more miles per hour. "You're sure a sloppy crook, Mr. Y, crashing into my wife. I'll bet the bakery has a security camera set up. By the looks of her heart rate and its quick recovery, it was a near miss. No harm done. Or maybe only a fender bender. Whatever it was, she's okay now. If any of the kids were in the car, they're fine, too, or her blood pressure wouldn't be so chill. Now the question is, was it an accident or intentional?"

Arlie went over the details of the morning's visit to Nero's home in his head as he drove past the flats. A lone moose was browsing in the swampy grass.

"Do we have a lone assailant or is this part of the De Luca family's revenge for the hassle Nero caused Papa years ago? Nah, couldn't be payback for Papa. There's no one left to fund a hit, and assassins don't do freebies. Plus, new guys looking to make a name for themselves go after someone recognizable, not a dough puncher in Witness Protection." He chuckled at the image. "Yeah, wannabes take someone out to steal his territory and scams, not his recipes."

Arlie's stomach gurgled at the thought of recipes and food. "I guess it's a good thing I'm already going to the Northern Lights Delights Bakery. Louie may love their apple fritters but right now, a big Bonanza Breakfast Burrito sounds like the perfect brunch."

Rather than let his mind wander about ridiculous scenarios like someone stabbing a man for his sourdough recipe, Arlie relaxed into domestic thoughts. He visualized a play yard for his three children. They loved the tire swing and playhouse that had come with the home when they bought it, but his family had outgrown it. More attachments were needed, especially since Louie and Rita's little LuLu was spending a lot of time with them now that they were backyard neighbors.

Before he knew it, he had arrived at the bakery. The aromatic combination of cinnamon, yeast, and bacon beckoned him. "Hey, Donna," he called out when he walked in.

"Well, good morning, Arlie." Donna wiped her hands on her

towel as she came in from the back. "Sweet or savory today?"

"I'll go for a triple B. Actually, you could call it a Four-B: Big Boy Belly Buster. It's almost impossible to eat one of those in one sitting!"

"So, I've been told," she said, a smile in her voice. She deftly slipped on a pair of disposable gloves and grabbed a huge tortilla. "Would you like me to cut it first and wrap each half separately?"

"Do you always have such forethought? Yes, please do. I fixed a peanut butter and jelly sandwich for lunch but since I had to drop by here anyhow, I figured I'd put it on standby. You know, in case I have an afternoon snack attack."

"So, why were you coming by?" Donna asked, spreading her special sauce over the huge spinach tortilla. "Did Charlene call you?"

"Why would she call me?" he asked, fishing.

"You didn't answer my question. I asked first."

Arlie sighed, watching her hand hovering above the bins of toppings. "No, she didn't call me. I guess if I don't fess up now, you'll go skimpy on the bacon."

"You're darned tootin' I would. So, since you answered me," she took out an extra helping of meat, "I'll tell you. Some guy almost backed into her in the parking lot. I thought he was a decent dude. He was asking questions about this place and how it's run. I think he's interested in buying us out. I told him to check back in a couple of months when it gets really crazy around here."

"And..." Arlie said casually, checking the display cabinet of desserts.

"And he was a big tipper. Had a major sweet tooth, too. He bought one of everything in there, plus half a dozen loaves of bread. When I asked if he wanted me to slice the bread, he said he had a knife and he cut good. Very good." Donna shuddered, recalling the gleam in the man's eye.

"What's wrong? You look like someone just put ice down your back."

"It's just the way he said it. 'I cut very good,'" Donna repeated, using the man's same Eastern European inflection. "He gave me the heebie-jeebies."

"From that accent you used, it doesn't sound like you think he was from around here," Arlie prompted.

"It wasn't just his speech. It was his little mannerisms. The way he abruptly opened the door, acted like he was doing me a favor by dropping in. He was a big tipper, too, and that's not like a local." Donna pulled the hundred-dollar bill out of her pocket and waved it at Arlie. "Biggest tip I ever got."

"May I?" he asked, reaching for it.

"Sure. Just make sure you give it back."

Arlie took the bill and held it up to the light.

Donna's excitement turned to frustration when she saw Arlie's twinkle of mischief dim to disappointment. "Dang," she huffed.

"Yeah, looks like you got stiffed. Can I keep it to see if there are others out there like it? Look-alikes usually come from the same source."

"Oh, double-dang," she groaned. "Yeah, you can keep it. He

bought the bag of bread and box of pastries with another hundred-dollar bill. I'm sure it's a phony, too." Donna opened the cash register, ready to grab it.

"Wait! Let me get it." He pulled out an evidence bag from his pocket. "If you don't mind, I'll take your prints and do a little subtractive reasoning. If I can get a set from one of these two bills, it might help. I can't get him for terrorizing my wife, but maybe I can put him out of circulation for passing funny money."

"Well, it isn't so funny when it comes out of your profit."

"Don't worry about it. There are plenty of opportunities for you coming up. You do cater, right?"

Donna's mouth twitched as she tried to tone down her smug smile of satisfaction. Adding catering to their list of products and services was her idea, not Paul's. "Yes, we do. It's not publicized – yet – until we can get a more reliable crew. Do you know anyone looking for a job?"

"If you don't mind guys looking for a fresh start, I can give you the contact information for Leon Lopez. He runs the Halfway House out of Palmer. He's very selective on who he lets on his crews."

"Palmer's close enough that transportation shouldn't be a problem. Yeah, take one of my cards and give it to him."

Arlie accepted the card, then asked the question he'd come in the door with. "Do you have any security cameras here? I'd like to see what this guy looks like."

"Yes, but I don't think they're going to help." Donna grimaced and pointed to two boxes on the bottom shelf behind her. "They haven't been installed yet."

Arlie's initial gasp at getting a break quickly sank into a low groan that he failed to contain. "Can you move it up on your to-do list? Maybe get one of your grandkids to put it up for twenty bucks?"

"I'll make calls right after I get done with your Bonanza Breakfast Burrito." Donna quickly folded and rolled the colorful creation into a fat pale-green tube, then cut it diagonally. *Whip, whip!* She grabbed two pieces of waxed paper and wrapped each half with practiced dexterity. *Whip-snap!* A medium-size paper bag was pulled out and opened in one motion, the two halves of the savory meal-in-a-wrap situated at the bottom with three paper napkins on top.

"As far as what he looked like, he reminded me of a fat version of that alien in the first Men in Black movie."

"Alien?"

"You know. He was a big bug that killed a hick and put on his skin?"

"The guy in the Edgar suit?"

"Yeah," Donna nodded, a grin of recall that quickly faded. "This guy was about six-foot tall, black hair that looked like he cut and colored it himself, and a pot belly. It looked like he lived on fast food and Twinkies. Nothing distinctive like a big nose, tattoos, or scars, but he did have a real big, bushy, black mustache. He was wearing a thread-bare, rumpled dark blue suit, like he'd been a lawyer or something but years ago. He moved as if he was uncomfortable in his body. That's what made me think of the alien in the Edgar suit. Then again, it might be he had a bum knee. Come to think of it, Paul moves just like that on rainy days." Her eyes brightened in pride. "Yeah, this guy has a problem with his left knee."

"Anything else?" Arlie asked, jotting notes in his little yellow notebook.

"Yeah. He must live alone. A woman wouldn't let her man out of the house in clothes that looked like he'd slept in them. Plus, he wore too much cologne, probably to cover his body odor. It didn't work. It just made him have spicy B.O. I don't remember the name of the aftershave or cologne or whatever it was, but it's an old scent. Guys in high school forty years ago used to wear it all the time. Yeah, I'd recognize his stink anywhere. That's all I remember. Anything else?"

Arlie grabbed a bottle of orange juice from the cooler and set it next to the cash register. "How about a little gift?"

She frowned and looked at the bottle. "Huh?"

"Not from you. For you." He pulled out his counterfeit-detection pen and handed it to her. "A better tip than a big bucks phony bill, right?"

She took the pen from him and chuckled. "I'd better take this before you change your mind." She keyed in his purchase and gave him the total.

"Meh. I don't need the pen anyhow." He gave her the cash and shook his head briskly, letting her know he didn't want the change. "I've seen enough counterfeit bills that I can spot one across the dining room of a mega restaurant. If I were you, I'd keep this clipped to the bib of your apron, highly visible. If you leave it here," he tapped the flat spot next to the cash register, "it will disappear. If you bring it out at the last minute, you'll put the crook in an uncomfortable and defensive position. It's best to keep him honest by wearing your fake-bill detector in plain sight."

"Okay. If I think of anything else, I'll text you. Oh, and I believe my prints are on file from when I applied for a federal job years ago. I'd rather not go through that again." She rubbed her thumb and fingertips together, pretending to scrub ink off them.

Arlie took out his phone, swiped and tapped a few times, keyed in her name, and said, "Yup. Got 'em. Thanks for the heads up. I'll let you know if I find anything. If we catch him, you might get your money back for the food…but probably not the tip."

"Hey, every little bit helps. Thanks."

Arlie set the juice in the bag and picked it up. "And thank you."

Outside, Arlie looked around the parking lot. There they were, just to the right of the front door – fresh skid marks where Charlene had braked to an abrupt stop when pulling into a parking place. He walked around, looking to see if anything had dropped out of Mr. Y's pocket or the car. He squatted down, hovering over the spot where the man would have gotten in or out of his car.

And there it was.

Green leaves and a stem.

Still intact and not driven over, a wilted sprig from a plant.

He picked it up. "Bleeding heart," he said softly, recognizing the variety. "And a rare white one at that."

He cradled his lunch sack next to his chest and grabbed another evidence bag from his pocket. "Probably nothing, but I've put someone at the scene of the crime with less." He put the botanical bit into the baggie, then set it in the paper sack on top of his brunch.

"Time for another visit to Abby."

Chapter 10: This Bag of Green or This One?

Anchorage
One hour later

Arlie pressed the security access button at Abby's lab. "Are you still hungry?"

"If you have food, I'll eat it." She held the open button. "Good timing. Come on in. I was just getting ready to call you. I may have found something."

"Me, too."

"Lunch and a leaf," he said when he walked in, holding up two mismatched bags. "Oh, and a hundred bucks says you can't get a viable print from this." He set the bags down and pulled out the other baggie from his vest pocket.

Abby took the one with the bill from him. "Do you know how many hands have been on this?" She held it up to the light. "Although this one appears fresh from the tumbler. It might only be a few people."

"That's why I figured you could get some good prints. It was given as a tip to a gal out in Palmer. Her fingerprints are already on file. I'll send you the link. If it was just the two of them who touched it, we're in luck."

"Okay, that one's pretty straightforward. What else do you have for me?"

Arlie took out half of the breakfast wrap for himself, then handed her the paper bag. "Oh, and this." He held out the evidence baggie. "You might want to get started on the green stuff first."

She clutched the spinach tortilla-wrapped sandwich with one hand, the top of the baggie with the plant sprig in it with the other. "Which one? They're both green. I assume you want me to analyze the plant, not the sandwich."

"Yes, the botanical. If there's something on the leaf, I don't want it compromised or washed away by plant juices or decomposition or whatever. Does it look familiar?"

"It looks like it came from that little white bleeding heart plant next to the big red one in Nero's backyard. I'd never seen a white and yellow variety before. Its fringed leaves were distinctive, though. Just like this one."

She quickly unwrapped the sandwich and took a bite. Speaking with her mouth full, she said, "I must be lightheaded from hunger. I'm not making any sense, even to myself. That'll teach me to eat sugar cereal for breakfast. Crash and burn two hours later."

"Do you need a hand with the diagnostics?"

Abby re-wrapped the sandwich, set it down, and brought out what looked like a glass dinner plate. "Nope. We got this. Come on, Buzz. I'll set this up in the clean room, so you can do your thing inside. You've had enough sunshine for today."

"Yes, Boss," the drone replied with a woman's sultry voice.

Arlie snorted in surprise and chuckled. He called out as she walked away. "Careful, Abby. If you get that thing too smart, she'll be your replacement. Downtown won't want someone who needs to stop and eat."

Abby set the plate on a nearly invisible pedestal in the small anteroom. "Nah, I'm not worried," she called back. "Someone still needs to program her, clean her sensors, paint her nails...er...trim. Plus, even if she can draw conclusions from the evidence she gathers, no one can ever replace human insight and gut hunches."

"Yup. And that's why our jobs are secure. So, you said you found something, too. What was it?" Arlie took a big bite of sandwich, then stuffed a stray piece of bacon back in his mouth.

Abby came out and shut the door behind her. "Buzz detected a very faint electronic signature when we first got there. I thought it might be noise from someone else's phone. Winifred's might be secure, but Louie's probably isn't."

Abby looked at Arlie to see if he had a response to her suggestion. If he suspected the same, he wasn't letting on. "Anyhow, whatever caused it has either been removed from the site or is completely out of juice. Zip. Zilch. Nada."

Arlie looked at the sandwich, decided against another bite, and wrapped it up. "Since Buzz is busy and she already checked that area once, I won't ask her to go out again. At least, not until she's done evaluating the leaf. I have a few, ahem, dozen phone calls to return. Plus, I need to get into 'clean up my to-do list' mode. Feel free to call me with findings on the C-note, leaf, or anything else. I still have the data from the first go-round with Buzz to look over closer, too."

He held up his smartphone. "And if that noise had been Louie's phone, it wouldn't have disappeared. Believe me, when his phone battery dies, everyone knows."

"Huh?"

"He whines." Arlie shook his head and took out his little yellow notebook. He started writing. "One more mystery to look into… I'll check in with you later."

"Okay. Now get outta here and let me eat. One of these days, I'm going to take a real lunch break."

Arlie grabbed his sandwich and saluted her with it. "Me, too."

***

"Hey, honey. I was thinking about working from home again later. Any chance I can have the den to myself?"

"Arlie, why don't you just ask if I have a book club or Wilderness Adventurers meeting today. Or garden club. Or play date with the girls. Or… Yes, you're right. It's easier to ask if the den is available. Yes, it is. I already made lunch for the gang, but I can fix you a quick omelet or sandwich if you'd like."

"No, no. I'm fine. I'll be there soon. I just need a change of venue. They painted a few of the offices down the hall. I don't want the fumes to get to me."

"No worries there. Just the same old *eau de* boys and babies here. I'll see you when you get home."

A minute later, Arlie pulled into the driveway. He coasted in the last twenty feet, so he didn't attract the attention of his sons playing in the backyard. He quietly shut the car door and walked around Charlene's minivan. It was parked outside of the garage. He looked down. Although it hadn't rained, he noticed the concrete was wet in places. Apparently, the boys had helped Mom today. An empty bucket with washrags hanging over the edges, drying, was by the faucet, the hose coiled up as best a six-year-old could.

"Or almost seven. How time flies..." He squatted next to the front bumper and ran his hand across it. No signs of impact.

"Looking for something?" Charlene asked.

Arlie bolted upright and turned to face her. His shock quickly turned to chagrin. "Kinda. Sorta. Maybe."

"No, he didn't hit me. Oh, I assume you saw something and are getting an up-close look to make sure I didn't hurt the car."

"Nope. I didn't really 'see' anything other than your heart rate go sky high. It recovered, so I knew you and the kids were fine. Or you and whoever was with you if there was anyone."

"Don't you trust me?"

"Yes...yes," Arlie sputtered. "I wasn't snooping on you at all. Trooper Andy put a tracker on a suspicious vehicle. I saw it almost crash into someone..."

"And that someone was me," Charlene said, her voice low and apologetic. "I'm sorry. It's been a day and a half already. For some reason, the boys have tons of energy today. I thought that having them wash the car would wear them out, but it seems as if it was just a warmup. Now they're in the backyard, digging a swimming pool."

Arlie raised an eyebrow.

"Or a compost pit. I just gave them a couple of garden trowels and told them to go for it. I wouldn't let them use shovels. They might actually get a pool dug if I did."

"So, back to the other subject. The guy who almost hit you. Or did he? I couldn't tell."

"No impact, no air bags deployed. Just a very loud couple of near curse words from inside the car."

"You're okay then?"

"Yes, I'm fine. Rita, the boys, and the girls were all with me. Come to think of it, it might have been those cookies that got them worked up. They only had one each. Then again, Rita gave them some of Louie's special homemade trail mix. I didn't look at how much or what it was made of. Knowing Louie, I'll bet it had both raisins *and* chocolate in it."

"They'll work it off. Now, did you get a good look at the driver?"

"What? Oh, no. Just a side view of a pompous dark-haired jerk with a huge mustache driving a big silver Mercedes. Or maybe it was a BMW. Whatever. It was a big, fancy foreign silver sedan. Real dirty, too. That might have been another reason I wanted my car clean." Charlene shuddered. "It was so close…"

He pulled her near and hugged her. "If you're okay, I'm going to sneak inside and start working. Don't tell the boys I'm here. They'll figure it out soon enough."

"Yup, they're like their father that way: born detectives."

Arlie looked at his car in the driveway, not close to the house but still visible.

Charlene took the hint. "Yes, they'll see it and know you're here if they come out. I think they'll stay in the backyard for a while. I sort of hinted that there was weeding to be done in front when they were done. I think they'll stay where they are until dinner."

"Works for me." He gave her a quick kiss, then hooked elbows with her. "Now let me get to work while the climate is quiet."

Arlie went into the den and put on his noise-canceling headphones. *Best Christmas gift ever, wife.* He caught a glimpse of Carlos in the reflection of the TV screen but kept his head down, not acknowledging his presence.

"Let's play ring toss outside instead," Carlos called back toward the kitchen. "We can play board games when it's raining."

"Okay," Chip answered. "But I'm gonna beat you again."

"In your dreams," Carlos said. He whispered, "See ya later, Dad," through the slightly open door, and then gently closed it.

"Great kid. Really great kid."

Arlie picked up a piece of scratch paper. He noticed the doodle one of the boys had drawn and flipped it over, giving himself a blank slate for pondering.

Nero.

Winifred.

Garden mess.

No security cameras.

No witnesses.

No weapon.

He went back and added the word 'smiling' in front of Nero and continued.

Or tried to.

He couldn't get the thought of that ornery Russian – or whatever he was – out of his mind. Dressed in an old suit, he wasn't a fisherman, firefighter, or farmer; slope-worker, chef, or salesman. A doctor or lawyer would have better personal hygiene. By wearing a suit in Alaska – even an old one – he was out of place anywhere but in a courtroom.

Is there a new player in town? Maybe an old foe of Nero's found him and just dropped in to stir things up. Or get revenge. Yes, that backyard encounter bypassed giving a warning and went directly to end game. Death by gut wound. This wasn't a robbery. It was personal. Payback. An emotionally charged vendetta.

Nero hadn't gone down without a fight, either. An argument first, and then a tussle in the garden. No, it was more than two men with bruised egos wrestling or shoving each other. Nero was fighting for his life. He loved his prize-winning garden, but peonies and bleeding hearts could be replaced. His life couldn't.

In the end, Nero lost. In those final moments, he had to know he was dying. Weak and bleeding out, the only retaliation left was to deprive his attacker of seeing him suffer. No doubt, he hadn't pled for mercy, either. Yes, Nero knew his assassin. He knew he was cruel and vicious. Without a conscience. Egotistical and self-centered.

Arlie's fists clenched, remembering his wife's earlier close encounter.

The murderer was the kind of guy who would buy a big box of pastries just for himself... and pay with a phony hundred-dollar bill. Leave a huge tip... but with even more bogus money. A man who would back up without looking... believing the world needed to watch out for him, not the other way around. Damage to the car wasn't his concern. It didn't belong to him. He would just steal another one.

Twice this mystery man, this Mr. Y, had made a negative impression on people he knew. Andy Adams had caught him racing down the highway at a felonious rate of speed. Donna got a case of the heebie-jeebies from him and was paid with counterfeit money. Mr. Y was reckless, without a care in the world.

Arlie's gut wrenched and he tasted bile. *And the second time, he'd come within inches of crashing into my wife.*

"Oh, knock it off, Arlie. Your imagination is going wild."

He glanced at his list, then folded it over. More than one piece was missing in this 'who done it' jigsaw puzzle. Or there was one component too many.

Winifred.

What part did she play in all of this? She said she didn't call 9-1-1 because Nero was in the Witness Protection Program. How did she know about that?

He chuckled. "She's sharp and figured it out by herself, I suppose. She may have taught me a lot of what I know but as she says, not all of what *she* knows."

He unfolded the note and looked at it again. "There wasn't a security camera at his place although I saw the mount for one. That's why she was out and about. She's been spying on him! Hacking into his security camera! When his feed stopped, she came to investigate.

"Or tried to.

"Properties and driveways in that Hillside neighborhood aren't known to be handicapped accessible. She panicked and called Jess and me to do a wellness check. By her pale features and flustered attitude, she didn't expect him to be dead. She lied. She told us there was a murder, so we'd come. She only feared illness or injury. His death was a surprise to her, too. Yes, she was more upset by his death than a retired agent should be."

Arlie held up his note again, then set it back down. "No witnesses," he said, doodling a little posey in the top right corner. "Other than the flowers in the garden and squirrels in the trees. The wildlife won't talk, but maybe Mr. Y left a little DNA in the garden. If it was him…

"Dang it, Arlie, stop trying to make that reckless, counterfeiting car thief Nero's killer. Stick to the facts, man."

He shook his head in frustration. "Back to hard data. Let's check the coroner's report."

Arlie skimmed over the first part, skipping down to the wound itself and Manny's speculation on what kind of weapon was used.

"Victim was impaled by a long, hard, sharp, round object with a pointed tip. No fragments of weapon were found. No foreign DNA. Two strands of reddish-pink thread approximately four millimeters long were inside the wound. These matched the color and composition of the cotton canvas fabric of the apron the deceased was wearing at the time of the attack. Death was caused by rapid internal hemorrhaging. Estimated time of death was approximately five minutes after stabbing. No suggestions on what caused the wound, but it did _not_ appear to be a sharp-edged blade."

He closed the laptop and sat back. "Not a sharp-edged blade but definitely a sharp-tipped one. One that didn't drip blood when he pulled it out. Or maybe he wrapped it in a cloth or put in a bag and mopped up the mess right away. Man, I hate tidy crooks."

CHAPTER 11: COMMUNITY SERVICE
OR DOES A BEAR POOP IN THE WOODS?

Nero's Backyard

"You know I could get arrested for this, don't you?" she said into the mic of her headset-camera combination unit.

"I'd do it myself if I could, Eddie," Winifred replied, trying to hide her frustration, covering it with a schoolmarm's near-scolding demeanor.

As always, Eddie was wearing camo-colored clothes. This time, though, she went further and slipped on matching cleanroom booties and a hair net. She was a six-foot mass of moving brown and green camouflage.

"What's that noise?" Winifred barked. "And why can't I see anything?"

"I'm covering up. You'll have to trust me. I'm not going to chance a hair falling out or leaving a traceable footprint. Now, just hush and let me do your job."

Winifred inhaled deeply, indignant at the disrespect, but didn't say a word. Edna 'Eddie' was right. Her former special ops student was doing her a big favor. Crossing a police line wasn't a hand-slapping offense.

The clomp, clomp of footsteps came through the microphone but Eddie wasn't talking. She'd never been into chit-chat.

Winifred bit her knuckle to keep from speaking. She was

overwhelmed with the urge to ask if she'd found something yet or suggest she look here or there. She took her hand away and instead crossed her arms and huffed, hoping the exasperation hadn't come through her mic.

Eddie replied with a grunted humph but didn't say a word.

Click.

It worked. Eddie grinned in satisfaction. Winifred had taken the hint and turned off her headset. The old lady was finally letting her take the lead on the 'boots on the ground' part of the unauthorized investigation.

A long five minutes later, Winifred saw her computer icon change. Eddie was online again. She switched hers back on and waited for the report.

"All I saw were the mounts for one camera in back and the hard wiring that led back to his house. There was only one set of footprints to and from the door. The assailant never entered the house but walked around back. He was driving a full-sized vehicle. Not a truck by the looks of the tire treads. Probably a sedan rather than a van. High dollar tires but Arlie probably has all that information in his report. What did you think I could find that he and his crew couldn't?"

"I won't know what it is until I find it. Or you find it. Maybe the wind rearranged the leaves covering a lost button or...or..."

"Or the camera you had me put up six months ago?" Eddie asked.

"Oh, shoot. Were you working for All-Secure Systems back then?"

"Yup. Still am. No trace of it or its components, either. There is the possibility that the assailant took the camera with him."

"Slim chance," Winifred said.

"Ah, I get it. That's why you were here. You had the feed going to you. When it stopped, you came by to see what happened."

Rather than reply to the supposition, Winifred gave one of her own. "Was there a reason why only one camera was installed? I thought those things always came in sets."

"They do. The old guy said he'd call later to have the others put up. He wanted to wait until the snow was gone and the ground had dried up. He was afraid the ladder would damage his prized perennials."

"Yes, that was Nero. He loved plants more than people. Wait. Let me amend that. It wasn't just plants, he loved *flowering* plants. He said they were proof that there was a God. Or something like that…"

Winifred paused and sniffed back unexpected tears. She hadn't meant to share anything with anyone when it came to Nero, especially anything he was passionate about.

When she found Nero last year after another one of the agency's last-minute relocations, she told him he'd have to find a pastime they could both enjoy. Gardening was a non-starter for her. She wasn't worth a darn in the yard. Tethered by disability to her scooter, she was limited to paved paths, unable to plant bulbs, or even pull weeds. They needed to find an activity they could enjoy together. Cooking or oil painting, maybe. With his past, he couldn't be a part of her newfound hobby: fighting crime with a bunch of little old ladies in capes. It wouldn't do for someone to recognize him.

"You know, I'm smarter than you think. I know you'll be able to walk again if you get that spinal injury fixed. You're just afraid of surgery, aren't you, sweetheart?"

A shudder went down Winifred's arms at the thought of knives, jolting her out of recalling his gentle chastisement. The warmth was replaced by the iciness of finding him lying on the ground, covered in plant debris, his features frozen forever in that eerie smile. His broad chest stilled…

"Well, if you aren't going to answer me, I'm signing off and going for a ride," Eddie blurted in frustration.

"Oh, I'm sorry. I was deep in thought. What was your question?"

"Did he have any friends besides you? I mean, I knew he had a business, but did he entertain at home? You know, barbecues, soirees, whatever with neighbors, clients, or maybe employees?"

"No, nothing like that. He worked out of his kitchen. Twice a week, a delivery truck came by to pick up the bread. Nero wanted minimal intrusions, and it wasn't just because he was in Witness Protection. He was a fanatic about his garden. He didn't want anyone around who could possibly step on leaves or disturb the blooms of his precious peonies or whatever else he had back there."

"Well, from what I could see, there was no forced entry into the house. Unless he kept valuables or drugs outside, it looks like the motive was vengeance, not robbery." Eddie paused and amended her statement. "Or someone just wanted to trash his garden. I'll bet it was beautiful in the summer."

"Yes, it was," Winifred said. "At least, it was last year."

***

"Hey, Uncle Louie," Chip hollered. "Come look at this. It's hilarious."

Louie came into the living room and sat on the sofa next to Chip. He reached out for the tablet. "Okay, let me see."

"Me, too. Me, too," Carlos hollered. "You were supposed to wait 'til I came back from the bathroom before watching any more of them."

"Sorry. Sort of," Chip said. He handed the tablet to Louie just as his brother slipped in between them. "Here. Start it from the beginning. I tell you, it's hilarious."

Louie hit play and the three redhaired men watched a young bear cub climb a tree, grab what looked like a tightrope with its front paws, and hang from it, back legs pumping like it was riding an invisible bicycle. Then, up went its back legs, too. Now all four paws clutched the wire. It 'walked' upside down, paw over paw, inching along until it got to its target: a bird feeder. An awkward batting practice ensued until the plastic seed and suet-treat contraption hit the ground. The bear dropped from his aerial perch and landed like a sack of flour next to it. He proudly rushed with his prize into the woods. Like a quarterback with a football, he was heading for his end zone, eager to eat the victory meal in his own domain.

The young men's laughter was so loud that it coaxed the frustrated Arlie out of the den. "Okay, okay. What's so funny?"

"Sorry, Arlie," Louie said. "I didn't know you were working

from home. I guess I should have looked out front for your car. I came through the back gate. But hey, since you're here, look at this."

Louie started the video over and handed the tablet to Arlie, waiting to see his reaction.

It wasn't the one he expected.

"Well, son of a gun," Arlie said. "I never thought of that."

"Huh?" the guys asked.

"This just gave me an idea. I need to go back to Nero's. There's something we didn't look for."

"What's that?" Louie asked.

"Scat."

"Huh?"

Arlie chuckled and shook his head. "I noticed a wire hanging loose from a pole at the edge of Nero's garden, where a birdfeeder may have once been hanging. If Winifred had anything to do with putting up security cameras, they weren't big ones. A seed-eating bear could have swallowed it while downing the main course."

"Yeah, that's a real bummer," Louie said dryly and shook his head. "I guess it's long gone."

Arlie grinned at Louie, waiting for him to pick up on what he had said.

"Scat? Do you mean bear poop? You're going over there to look for bear poop?"

"Yup. I'll be back later, guys. I'm taking my job on the road again...with extra gloves and evidence bags."

Arlie's two sons looked at each other then asked in a perfect imitation of Louie, "Huh?"

Louie's eyes widened and he cut off his impulsive offer to help. "Hey, you two. Let's stay here. Your dad's going into the woods to look for evidence that bears really do, you know, go poop in the woods."

"Ew!"

"Yeah, ew!" Arlie said, mimicking them. He handed the tablet to Louie. "Later, guys."

"I thought you were working from home today," Charlene said, coming into the room to see what all the excitement was about.

"I was until the guys gave me a clue about what to look for."

Charlene chuckled. "You mean these three gave you a clue about where to look for a clue?"

He gave her a quick kiss and added one to the forehead of the toddler in her arms. "Yup. It shouldn't take too long. I'll be home in time for supper."

"Yeah, Dad's going hunting for bear poop," Carlos said.

"Yeah, huh," chimed in Chip.

"And it was kind of mostly my idea," Louie added, wanting to claim credit.

"Does that mean you want to come with me?" Arlie asked Louie with a smirk.

"Nuh-uh," he replied emphatically. "I'll stay here with the guys and look for more inspiration." He swiped the screen of the tablet and typed.

Carlos read over his shoulder. "Funny bear videos."

119

"If you find anything, let me know," Arlie said, then gave Charlene another kiss and was gone, off to the woods near Nero's Hillside home to look for an intestinally processed camera.

He immediately thought of Winifred, the person who probably suggested – or insisted – Nero put up the security camera.

Had she already thought of it being hijacked by a bear and looked for it?

Stop being so competitive, Arlie. Who cares who catches Nero's murderer first? As long as he's caught, right?

He sighed deeply and got in his Outback. *She'll always be older but not necessarily always your teacher. Grow up and stop wallowing in that blasted 'always a student' syndrome.*

***

It was a pleasant drive. The tourists had left earlier in the day for the usual tourist attraction destinations. Only locals were on the highway now, speeding along, switching lanes just before the offramps with practiced precision. A quick flash of his turn signal and he'd joined a group of four to the Hillside neighborhoods.

Arlie parked three houses away, behind a big motorhome. No reason to advertise where he was. It was breezy and overcast, so wearing a camo windbreaker with a hood didn't look out of the ordinary. There was no reason to stand out with his bright red hair. Just as he was getting ready to step away from the car and walk to the greenbelt behind Nero's house, he saw it.

Winifred's modified 'handi-capable' van.

He stood back and waited, watching to see what she was up to.

She was waiting, too. Biting her knuckle impatiently, then slamming her hand on the steering wheel in frustration. She'd never been a patient person.

A few minutes later, her surrogate 'feet on the ground' arrived. Broad-shouldered and camo-clad with a full helmet to match, the rider moved as one astride the black Honda NM4 motorcycle, coming to a precision stop next to Winifred's window and pouting face.

Not much for stealth, that sleek ebony ride would turn heads everywhere. But with its speed and agility, it could catch up or elude capture, depending on the circumstances. Arlie only knew one person sassy and powerful enough for a ride like that.

Eddie.

Arlie grinned and nodded, watching her get off her motorcycle with the poise and command that said, "I got this."

'Good choice, Winifred. I can't think of anyone – other than myself – who could sneak in and out of a secure crime scene without being detected.' He paused. 'Then again, maybe Eddie could do a better job. I've never seen anyone so focused in my life.'

Eddie looked perturbed, said a few words, then disappeared into Nero's backyard.

Arlie wanted to hear what was going on, but guilt got to him. 'You wouldn't want her snooping around you, would you?'

A few minutes later, he could see Winifred was talking again. 'Damn straight, she'd listen in on you. She already set that up by giving that hat to Louie.' He aimed his genius phone towards the van, hoping to tap into the phone conversation. She was glowering, her head down as she looked at her phone.

Eddie's voice came in first. "From what I could see, there was no forced entry into the house. Unless he was known to have kept valuables or drugs outside, it looks like the motive was vengeance, not robbery." Eddie paused, changing her tone. "Or someone just wanted to trash his garden. I'll bet it was beautiful in the summer."

The frown on Winifred's face was heart-wrenching. Arlie was more certain than ever that she really did care for Nero.

"Yes, it was. At least, it was last year," Winifred said with a tone of nostalgia he'd never heard.

Eddie stuffed a wadded-up plastic grocery bag in the saddlebag of her Honda. She looked up and nodded farewell to Winifred.

Eddie had completed her mission The deed was done. She was taking any clean room supplies or gloves with her to be disposed of far away from the site.

It looks like Eddie didn't find anything. Either she or Winifred would have been grinning if they'd found the camera.

Or the murder weapon.

And then they were gone. Eddie's subtle single taillight heading further into the hills, Winifred's van's colorful caboose of geometric reds and ambers bouncing back toward Anchorage.

Now it was his turn in the woods. Odds were even that Winifred didn't have Eddie looking for bear scat. What she took away was treated like trash, not evidence.

Now it was time for 'doody' duty. He knew what he was looking for.

Arlie donned a pair of Neoprene gloves and stuffed a spare pair into his pocket, just in case one got a rip or tear. An oversized trash bag and claw-ended grabber completed his undercover attire of greenbelt cleanup volunteer.

It didn't take long to find the trail. It was used for both wildlife and for human 'wild life.' Whether he was being watched or not, Arlie picked up trash along the way. Empty candy bar wrappers, condom packaging, and a couple of empty beer bottles. Torn up and dog-chewed plastic flying discs, a few tennis balls, and enough empty soda and beer cans to smelt into a front door littered the area. And that was just within a fifty-yard perimeter.

Just beyond that, though, he found it. The ursine designated potty area. There was no mistaking the bear-clawed tree. He gulped, then realized these might be black bears in this neighborhood right now. The damage to the bark on their favorite 'scratching post' was less than five feet tall.

Lots of scat specimens were nearby. Rather than pick up all of them, he scanned each pile with his phone.

Tink. Tink. Tink.

"Bingo," he said softly as the last pile he checked emitted audible tones. "There's metal in this here scat."

Arlie held his breath. Using the edge of a discarded fast food hamburger box, he scraped the scat into an evidence bag. He double bagged it just in case it leaked. Ever so gently, he put it in his jacket pocket.

He sighed in relief. Stage one of his task was completed.

Arlie grabbed the filled trash bag and aluminum grabber and stood up tall. "I guess this takes care of my community service time," he said aloud.

Then he strutted down the path to his car. A bag full of trash picked up for the neighborhood and a pocketful of evidence-laden bear poop for him to analyze.

It was a very productive day.

Chapter 12: A Neighborhood Performance or Is He Just Plain Crazy?

Arlie's watch vibrated before he got to the end of the path. He looked down at the notification. It was an alert. One of his trackers was in the vicinity – within a hundred yards of him – and coming in fast.

The aqua one.

Mr. Y's car was so close that it was almost on top of him. Arlie turned tail and scrambled back into the woods. He spotted a thicket of wild roses and dove in the midst of them despite the prickles. Leggy and with few leaves, they would have to do. Even so, if he kept the hood of his camo windbreaker pulled close and didn't move, he'd be nearly invisible.

Arlie watched from his position uphill from the street. A silver Mercedes drove past Nero's house at a slug's pace. Someone was looking for an address or stalking.

Or maybe celebrating a victory.

The sedan pulled into the driveway across the street, backed up, and came to a stop directly across from Nero's.

Cool. The vehicle was perfectly positioned, as if the driver was posing, seated for a portrait.

Arlie held up his phone and zoomed in, video recording the car and the portly man behind the wheel.

The swarthy man's mustache was even bigger than Nero's but darker. No, not just darker, it was too dark. His weathered face looked at least fifty years old, but his hair and mustache were an intense but dull black. Lady Clairol charcoal black. Arlie looked closer at the man's features. He hadn't dyed his eyebrows. That's why he looked so odd.

Mr. Y suddenly smiled, then chuckled. His pensive laugh quickly erupted into an unsettlingly evil roar. Ravens and magpies scattered at the sound. Squirrels chittered at the noisy interruption of their scavenging routine.

The tone was hostile. Threatening.

A chill went up Arlie's spine. If this wasn't Nero's killer, then who was he? Why was he laughing so loud at the house? It was obvious something drastic – a tragedy – had happened there. The property was practically wrapped in yellow police line tape.

The continuous cackle stopped. The man took a breath. Rather than compose himself, he flung his head back. He paused – as if making a decision – then opened his mouth and howled like a wolf, revealing an unsettling amount of missing or blackened teeth.

Are you crowing in victory, Mr. Y?

A woman came out and stood on the driveway he'd used as a turnaround. She scowled and crossed her arms over her terrycloth bathrobe. Resolute. She was ready to chew him out. Mr. Y stopped his yowl and looked at her. Her eyes widened with fear, and she rushed back inside.

Smart woman.

The roadside performance of laughing and loud animal noises – wolves, coyotes, and roosters – continued for another full minute then

126

stopped abruptly. Mr. Y wiped his hand down over his mustache and sighed as he stared at Nero's house. Was he smiling in satisfaction or frowning? Arlie couldn't tell.

Finished with his zoological opera, Mr. Y reached toward the passenger seat, grabbed something, then sat back. He took a big bite of a full loaf of unsliced flat bread. He chewed it with glee. Bits of food dropped from his mouth as he chuckled, shaking his head minimally.

Buzz. Buzz.

Arlie looked down at his watch.

An alert had been sent. A 9-1-1 call had originated nearby.

Camera phone still focused on Mr. Y, Arlie looked over and saw the homeowner who had come out earlier. She was watching the show from her window. Phone in hand, she was probably still speaking with the dispatcher.

Get out of sight, woman!

As if she heard his urgent, non-verbal plea, the woman stepped away.

Ah, the dispatcher told her to keep out of view. Phew!

Mr. Y had seen her, though. He sat forward and looked around. A vehicle was coming toward him. He dropped his food, put the Mercedes in gear, and sped away.

He wasn't waiting to find out if it was a cop or not.

His sedan was out of sight in a flash, but Arlie knew where it was. He stopped the video on his phone and opened another app. Mr. Y's little aqua tracker was moving erratically. Stop, go, hard right, U-turn, back up, stop, a hard left, then creeping along.

Lost.

Mr. Y didn't have a clue to where he was.

No matter where you go, Mr. Y, you can't hide. While you're busy playing the game of mouse in the maze of Anchorage neighborhoods, I'll return to my office. I'm sure I can pull a good still shot from this video. A few minutes searching the databases, and I'll find out who you are. I'll know everything about you from your criminal record to your underwear size.

Arlie elbowed his way out of his thorny wild roses hideout and resumed his community clean-up volunteer persona. He strutted out of the woods, swinging his black bag of trash, whistling 'We are the Champions,' making sure he didn't hit his pocket loaded with bear scat evidence.

***

Once on the road, Arlie called Abby and gave her a heads up that he was on his way in.

"I hope you're bringing food. I'm so hungry I could eat a bear," she said.

"Actually, I do have a bit of bear. Not a whole bear, but I guarantee that no matter how ravenous you are, you won't eat this part, raw or cooked."

"Okay, I'll trust you. Do me a favor then and drive through someplace and grab me something to eat. Preferably something I can eat one-handed and that doesn't drip."

"A bacon, lettuce, and tomato milkshake?" he suggested.

128

"Grr."

"Why don't you eat that peanut butter and jelly sandwich I put in the fridge? Charlene has some sort of fancy press that seals the edges together. No grape jelly squirt outs."

"Perfect. This is Abby of Valley Vegetables and Vermin, signing off."

"That's so horrible, it doesn't even deserve a raspberry."

"Pbbt! And raspberries are fruits, not vegetables. I'm still trying to think of a name that won't attract bystanders. Even though it's been painted over, people still think it's an ice cream truck."

"Well, Abby, it was. How about 'We See You Tax Collectors'?"

"'Auditors Are Us'? Nah. I'm getting spacey. I'm gonna find that PBJ before you get here. I don't want you to change your mind."

"See you soon, then."

Fifteen minutes later

Arlie handed her a tall, frosty cup and a straw. "I figured a vanilla milkshake would taste better than chocolate after one of Charlene's peanut butter and grape jelly specials."

"Oh, thanks! Just what I wanted."

"Go ahead and enjoy your dessert drink. I'm taking over your lab for a few minutes to get started analyzing this."

"Oh, no you don't," Abby protested, punching the straw into the cup. "I get first dibs on anything that goes in there. I can delegate specific tasks later, but first shot always goes to me."

Arlie grinned at her as she lifted the drink and took a long sip. He pulled out the double-bagged scat specimen and waved it at her.

"First shot, you say? Does this mean you want first shot at shit, too?" he asked, stepping back.

She looked closer at the baggie contents and spewed a mouthful of vanilla shake.

"What the…?" she sputtered and scrambled for paper towels.

Arlie handed her the fistful of them that he had ready. "Hey, I'm pretty sure there's a security camera in there somewhere. Longish story, but I'm positive there's metal in this here dung. I found it in the woods next to Nero's."

Abby set her drink on the counter and finished wiping up her mess. "Okay. Now that I've seen the project, I'll let you have full control over the analysis of it. If there's something you can't handle, just ask."

"Will do, boss. Here's hoping digestive juices don't wipe out data on storage discs."

"I'll let you check out that part, too," she said scowling. "Now that I've lost my appetite and part of my milkshake, I'll put the rest of it in the fridge. I need to change clothes, too. Let me know when you have images available."

"As a matter of fact, when you're done cleaning up, could you check out something else for me? The file is in the cloud already. I uploaded a video thirty minutes ago. I need to find out who the guy in the car is."

"Who is he?"

"That's what I want to know."

"Arlie, you know what I mean. Where and why did you take the video he's in?"

"He was hanging out around Nero's house, parked in front, and laughing his head off. Actually, he started out laughing, then howled like a wolf that had just taken down a moose and was ready for the banquet."

"Ew!"

"You sound like my boys when you groan like that."

"Oh, and speaking of boys," Abby rolled her eyes, "Louie called. He wanted me to ask if you would call him when you got a chance. He was babbling something about not wanting to bug you at work since this was a personal matter."

"I think he wanted to make sure he didn't call when I was out looking for bear scat, afraid that for once I might ask for his help."

Arlie took out his phone and keyed in the number. "I think I'll give him a call before I get started. My mind will be clearer, not wondering what he's after this time."

He held up his hand as the call connected. "Hey, Louie. I'm back from the doody duty. What's going on? Okay. Well, did you ask Charlene if they could go? Oh, just Carlos? Chip's grounded for the afternoon? Why doesn't that surprise me? No, that's a rhetorical question... Rhetorical means I didn't expect an answer. You two go ahead. It's okay by me. I won't be back for another two to four hours, at least. Have fun."

Abby giggled as Arlie got more and more exasperated with the call. When he hung up, she said, "Sometimes I think Louie's a six-year-old boy in a twenty-six year old's body."

"And then he does something incredibly clever and surprises us all. Nah, he's just making up for not having a normal childhood. He wanted to take both boys 'taste-testing' finger foods for his wedding. Chip got in trouble and Charlene grounded him. Louie wanted to make sure it was okay if he just took Carlos with him. Charlene didn't want to be the heavy, so had him ask me."

"Sort of the parenting version of 'good cop – bad cop'?"

"Yup. I don't know how single parents do it."

Abby chuckled. "They're Super Moms and Dads. I ought to know. I had one. Now, back to work, Dad. It's not diaper duty, but it's close enough."

"Let's hope this inspired idea proves productive."

***

Twenty minutes later

Arlie disposed of all organic bits and pieces into the hazmat bag and tossed it into the receptacle. "Well, that was faster than I thought. It took longer to put on the personal protective equipment than it did to separate this little gem from the scat."

He held up the camera that was roughly the size of a quarter, eyeballing it for any obvious leftover contaminants. "Let's see what you can tell us, my little spybot."

Abby came in to join him, her drink in hand. "I couldn't find a match on the first run-through of your Mr. Y's image. I added in your algorithm that would take into account traditional plastic surgeries, different hair style, or weight changes. Any luck with your project?"

"Luck has nothing to do with it. Well, maybe a little bit. Have a seat and watch the premiere with me."

"All right!" Abby crowed.

Arlie ran the first minute of the surveillance video at normal speed, then fast-forwarded it. For weeks, there was nothing but lumpy piles of snow and icicle-draped eaves, shadows and quick views of chickadees, and an occasional raven dropping in to eat from the bird feeder above it.

"There he is," Abby said, reaching out to point at the screen.

The wide-angle lens captured Nero walking out his back door with a broom in hand. He quickly brushed a path to the edge of his porch, then stood there, peering out over his yard. He was wearing sweatpants, mud boots, a red flannel shirt, and a very contented smile. He turned and looked behind him. If there had been a noise, the camera hadn't captured it.

Nero opened the back door and grinned broadly as he held it open.

Winifred came rolling out on her red scooter, her smile as glorious as his.

"No wonder she wanted it back," Abby said.

"Suspicion confirmed. Two consenting adults are allowed to have a private life. Let's fast forward through the personal stuff."

"Agreed."

The pair's moment of romantic reflection was short lived. Winifred's shiver at a chill was followed by immediate action by Nero. He shrugged out of his flannel shirt, put it around her shoulders, then opened the door and let her ride back in.

By the time stamp, three more days passed without any activity other than birds checking out the Fly-in Cafe.

Then, two days before Nero's death, a different kind of activity started.

The still image of Nero's backyard started jiggling. At first, it was a minor up and down movement but soon progressed to intense vertical action, like a small ship at sea being tossed about on thirty-foot waves or a hyperactive teenager on a trampoline.

"The bear," Arlie and Abby said at the same time.

Suddenly, the sky filled their monitor. The boughs of evergreen trees and bits of birdseed dashed in and out of frame as the feeder and camera fell to the ground.

"Yikes!" Abby squeaked as a black bear's face filled the screen.

Arlie paused the video. "Thanks, guys," he said.

"Huh?"

"It was their idea. Or rather, they showed me a video of a bear knocking down a wire-mounted birdfeeder. Ready for more?"

"Duh. It just startled me, Arlie, that's all. Go ahead."

"Yeah, well, you'd better wipe your chin again. You're going to run out of work smocks if you keep spewing your drink like that."

"Grr." Abby grabbed a tissue, wiped the mess from her face, and nodded. "Ready."

It could have been any wooded trail in Alaska, but Arlie recognized the stand of wild roses he'd hidden in. The bear was toting the birdfeeder with the attached camera past it. Quick views of loose leaves, trees, and bushes appeared. Other times, the sky from a sleeping ground squirrel's point of view showed up.

Suddenly the two were face-to-face with a young bear.

"Eek!" Abby squealed.

Arlie stifled a gasp, hit pause again, and chuckled. "Yeah, well I was expecting it at some point."

"I'm glad I didn't have a mouthful when that happened." She scooted closer to him. "Play the next part real slow. I want to see what it looks like in a bear's mouth and, you know…"

"Going down its gullet?"

Abby nodded. "I know it sounds sick, but I'm curious if we can tell how long it takes to go through his digestive system."

"Yeah, well we know the end of the story."

"You mean the crappy ending?" Abby asked.

"I do love your sense of humor. Speaking of love," Arlie asked, "has Manny the mortician bothered you anymore?"

"Nope, but I did get some feedback from a few other ladies. I guess I was out of the loop. They hadn't thought about spreading the word via notes posted on the restroom mirror and stalls. I guess he's been hitting on just about anything."

Arlie started to push play and she stopped him. "Oh, and I should have the results from resurrected tissue sample anytime now."

"Huh?"

"The ones he threw in the trash and the janitor rescued. Plus, the ones I took after Manny closed out the coroner's report. I added them all to the pack and labeled it 'Abby's dog' in case Manny decided to intercept them."

"Great. Come on. Let's get through this. I want to see what that app came up with on our guy."

"Not my guy," Abby said. "If anything, Mr. Y's your guy since you were taking pictures of him."

"Abby, this is also the guy who nearly crashed into my wife's car with all my kids and a couple of my neighbors in it."

"Oh… I thought he was the murder suspect."

"He is. At least, he's leading me to think so. No matter what, he seems to have a fascination with bakeries and sourdough bread."

"I started to say you were just trying to pin something on a guy who endangered your family, but I see where you're going with this. Anyone hanging out in front of a dead man's residence and crowing has got to be weird."

"And stupid," Arlie added.

He clicked play again. Bright white teeth, a moist pink tongue, and then darkness as the camera was swallowed. Arlie fast-forwarded through the black, then clicked play when light appeared.

"What's that?" Abby asked, leaning closer to the screen.

They both sat back quickly at the raucous sound and rapid black and white movement.

"It's a magpie picking off undigested bits of birdseed, cleaning crap off the camera."

The image went shiny jet black and then dark.

"A raven drove off the magpie and flipped it over. No more video," Arlie said. "Even if she doesn't want any part of it, the raven doesn't want the magpie to have any, either."

"Listen, though. Is that someone talking in the background?" Abby asked.

Arlie cranked up the volume. They both got closer to the speakers. Nothing was distinguishable until a loud laugh.

"Louie," they both said.

He hit stop. "Yeah, we're up to the time we arrived for the body. I'll go ahead and enhance the audio, just to be sure."

Arlie noted the date and time of the conversation, then hit play again, fast-forwarding over the time they had both been there. When he got to the time they had left, he slowed it down.

Were those footsteps?

CHAPTER 13: A FRENCH
OR SOUTHERN ACCENT TODAY, SIR?

Same time

Carlos watched the mountains whiz by from his car window and noticed they'd passed the truck weigh station. He looked up and verified they were heading south. "Hey, Uncle Louie, are we going into Anchorage?"

"Um, well, kinda, sorta," Louie stalled. "I mean, since Eagle River and Chugiak are part of the Municipality of Anchorage, we've been there for almost two years."

"You know what I mean. I thought you weren't supposed to go into the city part of Anchorage for some big secret reason. I think I know what it is, though. So, why?"

"Why?" Louie asked, eyes on the road, his neck turning crimson in embarrassment. "Why are we going downtown, or why aren't I supposed to go?"

"Ugh. Do you have to play that game?" Carlos dramatically threw his head back in frustration, then tried again. "Come on. You were my pretend half-brother for almost my whole life. I know who you really are, who you were before you became Louie Lachlan. You're not supposed to be in Anchorage in case someone recognizes you as Lucky De Luca."

"Yeah, well, there is that..."

Suddenly bummed, Louie became quiet as memories of his old

life on the edge of crime popped in. Just as quickly, his perkiness resumed. "But hey, I'm not that same person, not really. I don't look the same now that my hair's grown out and I don't wear colored contact lenses. Shoot, I don't even talk the same. I don't cuss, and I'm a good dad and help fight crime with Arlie and Winifred and those crazy old ladies – I mean, concerned senior citizens – those caped crusaders. Besides, I don't think there are any bad guys left in Alaska who'd recognize me. They're all in prison or fled the country and can't come back."

"Well, just in case, you might want to put a pebble in your shoe and keep your hat on when we're there. Your face shape and expressions haven't changed, you know."

"Okay. But hey, what's with the pebble?" he asked as he turned into the midtown Anchorage bakery, the first potential caterer on his and Jess's list.

"It'll change the way you walk. I picked up a few hints over the years," Carlos said smugly.

"You're not even seven years old, dude." Louie put the car in park and unbuckled.

"Yeah, but those first five were really rough," Carlos said, wiping his eyes briskly, trying to erase tears, remembering his first mother who had been murdered.

Louie noticed the discomfort and got out of the car. He looked down at the gravel-dusted pavement, then bent over and picked up a small rock. "Will this one work?" he asked, holding up a quarter-inch-sized pebble.

"Yeah. Just put it in one shoe, not both." Carlos glanced up. "And put on your hat."

Louie grabbed the baseball cap Winifred had given him from the backseat and shoved it on his head. "How do I look now, nephew?"

"Just like Louie Lachlan," Carlos said with pride, wiping under his nose. "Just like my Uncle Louie."

"Well, let's see what 'horse divorces' they have for us to sample today, Carlos."

"Shorten it to Carl, just for now, would you? Oh, and I think you'd better stick to calling them finger foods. Your French accent is pretty bad."

"Finger foods and Carl. Got it."

Louie stood up, the micro boulder situated in the arch of his right foot. He took a step and flinched. "Ow," he whispered.

"Here, I'll get the door," Carlos said, stifling a giggle. "You look like one of your old lady friends at the senior center. It's okay. It just takes a little longer to get where you're going when you're old, huh?"

"Yeah, huh." Louie hobbled to the entrance, then stood up tall, adjusting to the discomfort. He took the door from Carlos and held it open for a woman leaving with two colorful cloth shopping bags of goodies. He tipped his hat. "Have a good day," he said with a fake Southern accent.

He stood beside Carlos at the counter and grinned. "Everything okay?"

Carlos rolled his eyes and shrugged. "Much better than the French accent, but maybe you better let me do the talking."

"But you're just a kid," Louie protested in a hushed whisper.

"Hey, I'm almost seven and besides, I'm supposed to be helping my uncle. Go ahead and sit down. I got this."

"Geez. Kids grow up so fast," Louie said and limped to the first empty table.

A middle-aged woman in a pink and white uniform waited patiently at the register. "May I help you, young man?"

"Yes, ma'am." Carlos looked at her name tag and added, "Miss Dolly. I'm helping my uncle select *hors d'oeuvres* for an event. He called ahead. I think it's under the name Louie Lachlan."

Dolly thumbed through her list of index cards with names and information and shook her head. "Is this for a wedding?"

"Yes, it is."

"Maybe it's under the bride's name," she said absently and went through the cards again, this time looking for the event theme. "I only have one wedding, and it's under the name Jess Ross. Is she the bride?"

"Jess is the other groom in the wedding," Carlos said with a big smile. "I'm getting another uncle. Cool, huh?"

Dolly chuckled and nodded, her face blooming crimson. "Yeah, cool." She pulled the index card and fanned herself with it. "Be right back. Go ahead and have a seat with your uncle. I'll bring over some plates, pens, and reference cards. I've found it makes selecting the right *hors d'oeuvres* easier if you rate them as you go along."

"Okay." Carlos turned toward Louie. "Did you hear that?"

"Yup. Come on and wait with me, Nephew Carl," Louie said,

patting the table in front of him, his forced accent making him sound like an ailing Colonel Sanders.

Carlos took a deep breath and sighed in exasperation at his goofy childlike brother-uncle-friend. He repositioned his chair to the other side of Louie. Now he could see who came in the door. His first mother had taught him to always be on the lookout. When Charlene, his second mother, couldn't understand why he was so fussy about where he sat, he explained that he always had to watch the door: for bad guys. His dad was a cop. He understood and told him thanks for being on the alert when he wasn't around.

Smack!

The explosive noise of a blunt force impact stopped all thoughts and conversations.

A fat man with a big, black mustache strode in. He had straight-armed the door, opening it with a near glass-shattering blow.

All heads turned and were now looking at him. By his broad smile, it was obvious the boor wanted the attention he'd just received. His noisy entry wasn't an accident.

Dolly peered out from the kitchen area, checking out the disturbance. "I'll be with you in just a moment, sir," she said, scowling at first, then segueing to a phony smile.

She returned to the back and came out with a large platter of assorted finger foods in various shapes and hues of white, tan, and brown.

"That is what I want," Yakov said, reaching toward the bounty.

She pivoted in place and gracefully moved around him to set the tray in front of Louie and Carlos. "There you go, sirs," she said with a genuine smile of pride.

"Thanks, Miss Dolly," Louie said, still using his Southern accent. He turned to Carlos and nudged him to say thank you, too.

Carlos was stunned – ashen and stilled – as if he'd just seen a ghost.

"Oh, don't worry about my nephew," Louie said, looking around quickly to see if he'd missed something. "He'll be feelin' as fuzzy as a bunny with its paw in a light socket as soon as he eats somethin'."

Louie's lame excuse for him brought Carlos back to the present. "Thank you, ma'am," he said. "These look delicious."

"Yes, they do," Yakov boomed. "I want plate just like that now. No, make that two. I'll eat one here and take one to go. I might need snack later."

The woman turned to him, completely unintimidated by his bossy attitude. "I'm sorry, *sirrr*," she said, dragging out the last part of the designation as if it was distasteful. "That arrangement was special ordered earlier. We custom make sandwiches to eat here or to take away. Our soups of the day and breads are listed on the blackboard. Other than that, if you don't see it on the shelves, it's not readily available."

"Why not?" Yakov asked, leaning close so they were now face-to-face, trying again to intimidate her.

Dolly used the back of her hand to wipe the modicum of spittle he had spewed from her face with an exaggerated flourish. "It doesn't matter why not. If you don't see what you like here, there are plenty of other places to eat in Anchorage. Now, if you'll excuse me, I have work to do."

When she turned to leave, everyone but Yakov breathed a sigh of relief and went back to what they were doing.

Except Carlos.

Head down, he spun the little cocktail wiener 'pig in a blanket' around and around on its little plate, his head down, but eyes focused on the entryway.

Louie started to ask what the matter was, then looked where Carlos was staring.

The reflection on the glass window showed Yakov strutting back and forth in front of the display of pastries and breads, the dip of each second step unique. The man had a noticeable limp.

A familiar gimp.

"Shit," Louie whispered. "What's he doing here?"

"Yeah, shit," Carlos whispered back. He took a bite of the wiener wrap and put the rest of it down. He looked to Louie. "I give this a four out of five."

Louie glanced at him and grinned. The boy had immediately jumped back into their role-playing game. "Let's see."

He took a bite and chewed, watching Yakov's reflection, making sure the hired assassin wasn't watching them. "Yeah, it'd be better with some honey mustard, but not bad. Let's see what else we have here. Nephew."

Yakov tapped on the top of the glass display case impatiently as the woman rang up the customer ahead of him. As soon as she was done, he bellowed, "I want one of everything that is sweet, plus a loaf of every kind of sourdough bread. Oh, and do you use wood-fired oven?

"Nope," she said bluntly.

"Hmph." Yakov looked at the delicacies and decided he didn't care how they were made. "Just curious."

"Before I box all this up, I want to make sure you saw this." She pointed to the handwritten sign taped to the display case by the register. 'No $100 bills.'

"Oh, no worries," he said. "I will buy a full hundred dollars of food. You not need to make change."

She shook her head slowly, glaring at him as if she knew what he had planned: passing a counterfeit bill. "No exceptions."

"Then I take my business to someone else," he huffed.

He turned and looked around the room again, eyeing everyone there who might have watched the exchange, seeing if he had lost face with them.

Nope.

The only ones left besides the server were the uncle and nephew eating the tray of goodies he'd wanted. Everyone else had left.

"Just as well," he said, standing in front of the door. "Real baker would use wood-fired oven only." He pushed the door dramatically – arm extended straight – and was spun around, as if the door had pushed back.

"It says pull," Dolly said dryly, suppressing a giggle.

A guttural growl escaped, and Yakov jerked the door open. He turned back to face Dolly. "Crappy bakery, anyhow."

All three of them watched as Yakov kicked the tire of his mud-splattered silver sedan in frustration, then got in and sped away.

Gone.

"Are you okay, Miss Dolly?" Louie asked, all traces of his feigned accent gone.

"Yeah, I'm fine. I grew up on the east coast. I thought I was done with ass... with creeps like him. I guess bullies are everywhere." She looked down at the platter of food her two patrons had barely touched.

"I think you guys need something to drink to help that go down. Let's see, coffee, milk, or soda? I can make thirty-one different flavors?"

"Of milk?" Louie squeaked.

"I think she meant sodas," Carlos whispered. He looked up at her. "Yes, I'll take a plain milk, please."

"Oh, and maybe I'd better stick with black coffee. This is a lot of food." Louie blanched, remembering he hadn't been using his fake voice. "I mean, this is a lot of food, ma'am."

"Don't worry about eating all of it now. I can box it up and you can take it home. Your fiancé might want to try some, too."

Carlos elbowed Louie. "Can we forget about the drinks and go home now, Uncle Louie? I kinda lost my appetite."

Louie looked at the woman. "Yeah, I guess that would be a good idea. Sorry to be such a bother." He quickly added, "Ma'am."

"No problem. He made my stomach turn, too."

The two men waited silently at their table while Dolly packed up the finger foods in the back. Both were too stressed about seeing a fiend from their past to say a word, even to each other.

Two minutes later, she set the box in front of them. "No charge. It looks like Jess prepaid when he ordered it. Oh, and these are for you, too." She set two peppermint candies on top of the box. "Maybe they'll help settle your tummies."

"Thank you, ma'am." Louie took one and handed the other to Carlos. "Let's go home, Carl."

Louie stepped outside and looked around. Great. Yakov wasn't in sight. "Coast is clear."

Carlos came out and double-checked, just to be sure. "Okay."

Louie set the box of food on the hood of the Jeep and opened the door for Carlos. After he made sure he was buckled up, he threw his hat on the seat beside him. "We'll be home in just a bit, but I have to call your dad first."

"Okay. Don't forget the food, though." Carlos pointed to the pink box, setting cattywampus on the hood.

"Oh, yeah." Louie grabbed it and absentmindedly set it on top of his hat as he fumbled in his pocket for his smartphone.

"Found my phone!" he said and settled into the driver's seat. A few taps and swipes later, his call was placed.

"Hey, Arlie. This is me, Louie. Your neighbor and kinda brother-in-law. Oh, yeah. You probably have caller ID plus you know my voice. Anyhow, don't get mad, but Carlos and I came to Anchorage today. Remember you told me it was okay if we checked out finger foods for the wedding? Well, I wasn't sure if you knew it or not, but the bakery was in Midtown. No, I never said it was in the Valley…

"Hey, but anyhow, I need to tell you, Carlos and I saw a really bad creeper at the bakery. The dude was from my past. Oh, and Carlos's past, too. We were real careful while he was there. I used an accent and everything. Carlos gave himself the alias of Carl and I was just Uncle. We were both in disguise. Well, not Carlos because he doesn't look the same as he did when he was a four-year-old kid. Anyhow, the guy was Yakov. I never knew his last name and he never got a nickname like Hugo the Huge or nothin'. Since he was the only Yakov around, he didn't need more than one name.

"Yeah, well, anyhow, I thought I'd call and let you know about the big-time creeper in town from our past – Carlos and me. He's kinda, sorta one of the bad guys Papa De Luca hired to take out Carlos when he was a kid. I'm pretty sure he's not after him now, though. Even if he knew who Carlos was, I think that contract went away when Papa got sent to the slammer. Thanks again for putting him away. Oh, and he was never after me but knew I was Papa's son, even if I really wasn't. That was when I dyed my hair black and wore brown contact lenses."

Louie reached up and felt for his missing hat. "Oh, and I was wearing the hat Winifred gave me the whole time we were at the bakery, just in case. It was part of my disguise. Wait. What? You think so? You mean you think maybe she put a spy camera in mine like the one you put in Jess's See-Hawks hat? Okay. I can bring it over and let you look at it when you get home tonight. Yeah, we'll be extra careful coming back. See ya."

Louie pulled his smartphone away from his ear. "Man, your dad sure likes to talk a lot."

Carlos replied with a stifled groan.

Louie looked back at him. The boy was slumped forward, his face in his hands,.

"Are you sick?"

"No, I don't think so. But do you think he recognized us, Louie?"

"Not a chance. He's not too bright, at least not smart enough to act like he didn't know us if he really did. I would have seen it in his face if he had. Plus, like I said, neither of us looks the same. You don't know it, but you've grown up a lot since you were a kid."

Carlos sat up with renewed confidence. He rearranged his seatbelt with pride. "Yeah, plus he wasn't looking for us. Still, I wonder what he's doing in town."

Louie started the car and pulled into traffic. "I don't know either but when we get home, maybe your dad will have it figured out. He always knows what to do."

"Yeah, but was Dad mad that you went to Anchorage?"

"Well, maybe a little. But you know, Jess wouldn't have paid for that food if he didn't think we were going into town to at least pick it up."

"I guess you're right. Since he's FBI, I think he kind of outranks my dad." Carlos grabbed his water bottle out of the cupholder and took a sip and yelped.

"What's wrong, Carlos?"

"Nothin'," he mumbled then looked at Louie, watching him from the rearview mirror. "Well, maybe Mom's right. I think I have a cavity. I don't want to go to the dentist, though."

"Hey, I got an idea." Louie flipped on his blinker and made a hard right turn. "See where we are?"

Carlos looked out the window. "Yeah. That's the building where Abby works."

"Let's go see her. I'm sure she has some sort of microscope or something that can look in your mouth. She can check to see if there's a cavity without all the chains and bibs and spit suckers and shots they use at the dentist's office."

Carlos paled at the descriptions of all the implements. "Okay," he said meekly.

Louie pulled into the parking lot. "Hey, maybe she has some kind of super glue to patch up the hole, too."

Carlos mumbled, "Okay," and unbuckled.

Louie let Carlos out and started to shut the door, then stopped. He fumbled under the box of bakery goodies and grabbed his hat. "I don't want to forget you."

***

Arlie fast-forwarded through the hacked video files from Louie's hat and confirmed what he suspected.

"Bingo. Or maybe I should say, 'Yingo.'" He captured a still from the video feed and compared it to the one he'd taken of Mr. Y in front of Nero's home.

"So, Mr. Y is really Yakov Putin, the illegitimate son of a soviet era KGB agent who went independent. The first question, Yakov, is

151

why are you in Anchorage?" Arlie hit print and made a hard copy of the two images side by side.

"And the second question is, why are you *still* here? If killing Nero was your job, why hang around?"

Bzzz. Bzzz.

Arlie looked at his watch and saw Winifred was calling him. He tapped the watch face and answered the call. "So, you saw him, too? Who is he to you and/or Nero?"

"You used to have decent telephone manners, Arlie. What happened?"

"You proved to me they were a waste of time, jabbering useless cordialities when you could be getting down to business. Now, I was polite and answered your question without you answering mine first. Do I have to repeat it, or do you remember what I asked?"

"Tsk. Yakov has had an unrequited crush on Nero for years, decades maybe. He found him in Anchorage just after I did. Evidently, Yakov was spurned one too many times. If he couldn't have him, no one else could, either."

"Winifred," Arlie asked gently, "Do you think that maybe he was tracking you and you led him to Nero?"

"Oh, crap..." Winifred gasped, then put the phone down, overcome with guilt.

Arlie picked up his smartphone, tapped the hyper-audio button, and heard her sobbing. He cancelled the app, and waited on speakerphone, letting her compose herself in private.

"Hey, um, not to be callous, but even if that were true – and I want to assume Yakov's not that bright or you're not that sloppy – why is he still hanging around?"

"Oh, my. You're right, Arlie. He's not done with what he set out to do. Do you think he's after someone else?"

Arlie didn't want to think it was Winifred and didn't suggest it. If she hadn't thought about that already, she would soon. "Don't worry about it for now. Hey, thanks for telling me about Yakov's crush. At least some of it makes sense now. As we both know, jealousy is one of the top motives for murder."

"Just after money," Winifred said.

"Yeah. Well, hey, I gotta go. Abby has some DNA samples brewing and I'm eager for answers. I'll give her a heads up about Yakov. There's no doubt the guy in both images is the same person. If Yakov's creepy little chromosomes are in the database, it might shorten her search."

"Okay. And keep me posted... Hey, wait," she exclaimed, her snarky attitude back, the weak, weepy woman gone. "You said you have two images. Where'd you get them?"

"I don't have time to explain," he said. "But just a hint: Louie really likes that hat you gave him and so do I. He wears it everywhere."

"But...but..."

Click.

Winifred fumed at being hung up on. "Damn it, Arlie. So, you figured out how to hack the feed from Louie's hat. Where and how did you get the other image?" She paused, then asked herself, "And why were you looking?"

CHAPTER 14: INDIGESTION
OR INTENTIONAL INFILTRATION?

Ten minutes earlier at Winifred's home

Winifred put her spare readers on top of her bifocals. Leaning forward, she looked closer at her computer screen and the live feed of audio and video from Louie's Chinooks baseball cap. "Well, I'll be whipped and dipped and topped with strawberries. It looks like Yakov's back in town. And with a new nose and at least fifty extra pounds."

She took a screenshot and continued to watch one of Arlie's sons go green in the gills.

"Shit," Louie whispered to him. "What's he doing here?"

"Yeah, shit," the youngster replied. He took a deep breath and looked at Louie, his composure renewed. He picked up his funny-looking finger food, took a bite, and gave it a rating.

"What in the hell?" Winifred couldn't believe what she was seeing. "Is this kid an actor or some sort of child prodigy? And why would he know who Yakov is?"

Winifred jotted questions on her deskpad, not taking her eyes from the monitor as she studied the bakery and its occupants through the camera in Louie's ball cap.

Why Y at bakery?

Why L and kid know Y?

Why L talk funny?

Two minutes later, the excitement was over. Louie and Arlie's son were back in the car. Louie had tossed his hat in the back seat. Concerned about the boy, he hadn't noticed that he'd set the pink box of finger foods on top of it.

No more visual and only garbled audio.

Winifred sat up straight and twisted her neck. The show was almost but not quite over. "Not much to see but still more than I would have without my little 'fly on the wall' hat. Beat that, Arlie Biggar."

***

Intent on monitoring Louie's surroundings and conversations, Winfred hadn't noticed the incoming call from Arlie, her phone set on vibrate and still in her purse.

Arlie put his phone back in his pocket. "So much for showing a little professional courtesy, Winifred. Abby just gave me all this sparkling new data. I'm sitting here, waiting for your spin on what it could be, and you won't even answer my call. Let's see if I can read between the parts per million and find out how Yakov…"

Arlie shook his head, physically trying to erase any prejudices he had about who Nero's killer was. "Gut feelings are one thing. Hard facts are needed to get search warrants and make arrests."

***

Louie led Carlos up to the receptionist. "Hi. This is Arlie Biggar's son, and we're here to see Abby. I…um…forgot her phone number. Could you buzz her and tell her Louie and Carlos are here to see her? It's kind of an emergency."

157

Carlos pinched his thumb and forefinger together and gestured to the woman. "An itty-bitty emergency," he said softly.

"Let me check and see if she's available." She called Abby's line. "I have a couple of young men here to see you, Abby. One of them is Arlie's son. Which one? Oh, I'm not sure."

"He's Carlos and I'm Louie. He's Arlie's son, not me."

The receptionist rolled her eyes and grinned. "Oh, you heard that? Okay. I'll have them wait here for you."

Louie raised his hand and called out toward the phone, "I heard that, too. Thanks, Abby."

A minute later, she was there. "Carlos! Louie! What can I do for you? Oh, wait. Let's go to my office. We'll have a little more privacy."

Once they were at her workstation, Abby got serious. "What's going on, Carlos?"

"He's got a toothache," Louie said.

Abby turned to Louie and scowled. "Is your name Carlos?"

"Oops. Sorry. Go ahead, Carlos."

"Can you see if I have a cavity? My tooth hurts when I eat something real cold. I brush my teeth twice a day and floss and…"

"And?" Abby prompted.

"And Louie kind of scared me about dentists. I never saw one."

"Never? You mean, your mom never took you to the dentist?"

"No. She only took me to the dental hygienist. They're always ladies which is good because their hands are smaller. But since you're a girl and your hands are smaller, too, would you take one of your

158

spybots – or whatever you have – and look and see if I have a cavity? Louie said you might have some kind of glue or something to fix it. I don't want spit suckers or drills or any of that other stuff in my mouth."

Abby looked at Louie and huffed in exasperation. "Stop scaring kids, Louie." She looked back down at Carlos. "Things have changed since he was a kid. Come on and let me take a look."

Louie started to follow them into the back, but Abby stopped him with a glare. "Wait here and don't touch anything. We'll be right back."

Louie folded his arms and plopped down on a hard plastic chair. He crossed, then uncrossed his legs several times, then put his hands on his knees, trying to hold still. He stood up and walked around the chair, holding onto the back of it, making sure he didn't touch anything else. Frustrated that he didn't have anything to do with his hands, he ran his fingers through his hair.

Or tried to.

He was still wearing the hat. He took it off and tossed it on top of the file cabinet. "There, that's better." Louie pushed his fingers through his longish red curls, tucking them behind his ears, then bringing them forward again. "I forgot what it's like not to have anything to do. I guess being a dad keeps me busier than I thought."

"Hey, Louie!" Carlos called out, rushing out of Abby's private office with a big smile. "She fixed it. And get this: it wasn't a cavity. I broke a tooth. She fixed it, too."

"Huh?"

Abby followed Carlos out of her office and explained. "He chipped a baby tooth. It was a molar and would be coming out of his mouth in a few years anyhow. Many dentists would have pulled it rather than repair it."

Louie's eyes widened, and he started to babble, "But...but..."

"Don't worry about it, Louie. My dad was a dentist. I learned a lot just being around him. I know how to fix little stuff like this. I used to fix chipped teeth on friends in college. I always have some super epoxy on hand here. I just made a temporary crown for him. Temporary as in it's good until the tooth falls out on its own."

"And look at this." Carlos opened his mouth wide and pointed. "I got a purple tooth!"

"He wanted a red one, so he'd look like a vampire." Abby shook her head. "All I could think of was how freaked out Charlene would get, at least the first few times when he opened his mouth and she saw blood. Or thought she saw blood."

"Yeah, but now I can tell Chip that I'm a vampire who only drinks alien blood."

"So, are you two good?" Abby asked, gently urging them to the door ahead of her. "I have lots of work to do."

"Oh, sorry about barging in," Louie said.

"No, that's okay. This was an emergency. I'll escort you downstairs. Don't drink anything hot or cold for two hours, Carlos. If you're real thirsty, you can have sips of tepid water."

"What's tepid?" Louie asked.

"That's like lukewarm," Abby said.

"Don't worry, Abby. I just won't drink anything for a while, just to be sure. Thanks again. Oh, and thanks for telling me about your dad. He seems like a cool guy."

Abby knelt beside Carlos. "Take care of Louie, would you? Make sure he doesn't make a habit out of coming down here. You never know who's going to show up from his past and recognize him."

Carlos paled and nodded, thinking of Yakov. "Yes, ma'am. I'll try."

***

Ten minutes later

"Hey, Arlie. Come on back."

"What's going on, Abby?" Arlie asked. "I feel like I'm hiding from someone."

"About that in a minute. First, I want to give you a heads up. I just fixed a broken tooth for Carlos. Did you know he and Louie were downtown?"

"Downtown?" Arlie grumbled. "I was sure he told me they were in Midtown."

"They were. They made a detour to see me for emergency dental repair work. So, why we're talking back here is because Louie left that cute little spy camera hat that Winifred gave him on the file cabinet out front. I'm not saying anything important around it. I thought you might want to know about it in case you wanted to feed her some information without actually telling her."

"That might work. She's sharp and insightful, but still a private citizen and no longer associated with any law enforcement agency."

Abby chuckled. "Yeah, other than hanging out with those crazy old ladies who made the news a few months back. I guess the colorfully caped crew is still making the rounds. They don't catch anyone doing more than littering or parking illegally, though."

"Hey, by just hanging out in the neighborhoods, they're a deterrent. Thefts and vandalism are down. Sometimes those elderly activists are a nuisance but other times, their complaints generate leads that give officers a foot in the door. So, on another note, how long until you have those DNA samples cooked, coded, and cross-referenced?"

Abby jiggled the mouse, waking up her computer. "I'd say less than an hour. I did discover one thing for sure. My samples and the ones Manny took and then discarded were not from the same person. Someone needs to give Henry the janitor a bonus or promotion or something. What Manny did wasn't just negligence, he was intentionally obstructing an investigation."

"Wow. That's a pretty serious allegation, Abby. Are you sure you aren't a bit prejudiced because he was hitting on you?"

"Um, no. Jerks are all around. Guys who are in positions of authority and use their certification to mess with the system are beyond jerks – ultra-jerks, maybe?"

Abby's caustic attitude suddenly turned serious. "Arlie, I'm pretty sure Manny took the samples from himself."

"How do you know, and why would he?"

"How? Um, because when I tested the 'under the fingernail' samples, a unique compound came up."

"I'm listening…"

"I found my super-duper hand sanitizer, the one I developed which is only available in this building and at my house. It's unique. There was a high concentration of it in the sample. Manny was wearing gloves, so it's not contamination. Everything else I found was the usual – skin cells, body mites, that sort of thing. He only wanted the samples to *look* like the right stuff. I know he took scrapings from Nero because I watched him do it. He must have taken the ones from himself later, after I left."

Arlie chuckled. "Yeah, then tossed them in the trash, not realizing Henry would find them."

"He took the real ones with him, I'm sure. I'll bet he claims the courier lost them," Abby said.

"I know, that's what I'd do," Arlie said. "So, that leads us to the second question: why?"

"That's your job to find out. My stab in the dark guess – oh, bad analogy – is that Manny knows who the murderer is."

"Dumb crook." Arlie shook his head.

"Huh? I figure he's just an opportunist government employee who saw a chance to make extra money on the side by using the real samples as blackmail material."

"Abby, criminals who've been around a long time are either very smart or very lucky. If I were a crook and Manny tried to blackmail me with that stuff, I'd tell him to go ahead, release the test results. He'd be the one in trouble. Interfering with an investigation, theft of key evidence… The list goes on. Manny's looking at long jail times for those crimes. He's not too bright the way he's operating or it's not money he's after."

"What else is there?"

"Positioning, a part of the action. If he can prove to the right – as in bad – people that he can be of value to them by working on the inside – protecting them from prosecution by exchanging or disposing of evidence for a price – he has a shortcut to getting his street creds and making big bucks down the road."

"A perpetual stream of clients to extort," Abby said. "Geez. Oh, and I checked the international DNA records. Somehow Manny's DNA record isn't in either the employee or criminal database. He's a ghost, Arlie. He's either been doing this a long time, or he's wanted to. Anyone who works with sensitive material is asked to give a DNA sample. In case there's contamination, the agent's and technician's DNA can easily be excluded."

Arlie nodded. "So, in this case, Manny's DNA is the only one? If there's no record of it, how are we going to prove he did this?"

"Like I said, Arlie. That's your problem. But before we get too wound up with Manny, let me tell you what I got from the samples I took."

Arlie realized they were behind the privacy door and out of earshot of Louie's spy hat. "Is this something we want to share with Winifred?"

"Having another experienced investigator working on it wouldn't hurt." Abby changed her voice and attitude and stood up. "Let's review this information with my laptop. I think it's a little hot in here today, don't you?"

Arlie led the way out of her office to the conference table. "Let's work out here, Abby. That pizza I had for lunch didn't agree with me." He tucked in his chin as if stifling a burp. "Believe me, I'm doing you a favor."

Abby set her laptop on the table, resisting the urge to position it so it was pointed toward the camera in Louie's cap. Winifred would just have to work with what she got from whatever angle Arlie used to view the computer.

"Let's see here," Abby said, opening the file. "As I was saying, my samples and Manny's samples don't jive. Manny took the ones he tossed in the trash from himself and no telling where the other ones are."

Arlie squirmed in mock discomfort, posturing for another revelation. "He probably still has them with him or locked away in a safe place. I don't know what he's going to do with them unless he has a DNA lab that's as good as the government's."

"He could use a private one, couldn't he?" Abby asked.

"Yes, but those take up to two months to culture and grow the DNA samples that our guys can process in a fraction of the time. So, let's ignore anything he did with the ones he kept and concentrate on the ones you took later, okay?"

Abby chuckled. "So, he has blackmail material. He could release the real samples and results if he didn't get what he wanted from the murderer, whether it was money or a part of the action."

"Ugh," Arlie grunted, pretending to belch. "But he didn't. Score one for the good guys if we can prove it."

"That'll be tough. First, they'll have to catch him with the real evidence. Just because it's missing doesn't mean he did something wrong. He could claim it was lost in shipping or that the janitor had something to do with it. Manny doesn't know I took more samples. When the results don't come back, he expects someone to ask him when he shipped them out. He can say Henry volunteered to drop them off that day but must not have. He's already set up a patsy."

"Yup," Arlie agreed. "Manny's either very smart or very dumb. All he had to do was tell Nero's murderer that he had the evidence to put him away. He didn't even have to show it to him. His position as the presiding coroner would be enough."

"So, whether he's a genius or an idiot, I don't care." Abby wafted air in front of her nose, frowned, then continued. "As far as test results, this is what I have. Under the real Nero's nails, there's a minute amount of garden soil. He was wearing gloves in the garden or there'd be more. I'd say that trace amount was contamination from putting on dirty gloves."

"You must have found more than that, though."

Abby inhaled deeply, ready for the zinger. "Oh, yeah... A considerable amount of Yakov Putin's DNA was on Nero's cheek. He either gave him a big, slobbery kiss or licked him."

"Ew!"

"Yeah, ew," Abby repeated. "Why would that be?"

"Well," Arlie said, waiting for Abby to look at him. "Winifred did tell me that Yakov had a crush on Nero. If he had him in a compromising position, he might have…er…um…stolen a kiss."

"There's no telling if it was before or after he died, though. However, by the smile of 'You're not going to make me cry or beg for mercy' on Nero's face, I'd say it was after. Yakov sat there and watched Nero die, hovering over him in his last moments. Nero was one tough, ornery cookie."

"I'm sure Yakov watched but for how long, we'll never know." Arlie added, "Unless there's another camera out there we don't know about. Hey, what about that plant leaf I gave you?"

"It was just a leaf from a white bleeding heart. It's not that common, but even around Anchorage, it's probably in over a dozen gardens. However…"

"Don't keep me waiting, Abby."

"Hai Karate," she said brightly.

"'Lo, Jiu jitsu."

"No, no. You don't understand. Buzz picked up the same unusual chemical scent both in the garden and on that sprig of bleeding heart. You're right. That ties them together. Arlie, it's a cologne. Hai Karate was popular back in the 70s and 80s. I didn't even know they still made it. It might be rare enough…"

"Hold on. I'm pretty sure that's circumstantial. And now for my however… Donna said the man who passed the phony hundreds reeked of an aftershave popular when she was in school. That makes sense. Do me a favor. Check those bills I gave you for the same scent."

"I'm one step ahead of you. Done and yes, they're the same. The cologne isn't the only marker, though. Buzz does medical diagnostics, too. She detected what you and I would call a fruity scent. It often indicates diabetic ketoacidosis."

"How precise is the aroma data Buzz picks up? Is it as consistent and unique as DNA?"

"Not yet, it isn't," Abby said, pouting. "That's something I'm working on, though. Animals can recognize people and other animals by their scents. I just haven't figured out to mimic that talent, isolate the markers they use, digitize them or…"

Arlie put his hand on hers. "Give it time. I'm sure if anyone can do it, you can."

"Or we can," she said and winked. "Buzz is *our* creation, after all."

"Agreed. Now, what bothers me most is that I still can't figure out what weapon he used."

"According to every test I could think to run, there wasn't a trace of metal, glass, ceramic, or wood around his wound. It was pretty much just Nero's own blood."

"Well, without a weapon and nothing more than a kiss on the cheek of the victim, we don't have squat. A lawyer could say the two had a lover's spat, wrestled in the garden, and then Yakov went on his way, a plant leaf stuck to his shoe. His tire tracks and shoe prints could put him at the scene, but there's still no weapon. It looks like our prime suspect, Yakov, is getting away with murder."

"Dang. That sucks."

Arlie feigned a groan and pushed Abby's laptop toward her.

"Hey, if something else comes up, let me know. I have to find some antacids."

Abby opened her mouth, ready to tell him she had some in her desk, then realized he was just closing out their performance for Winifred. "Okay. I really don't have anything else. If something comes up, you'll be the first to know."

Arlie stood up and pulled his shoulders back, wincing in mock discomfort. "Oh, and I have an audio specialist coming in to work on that bit of camera noise recorded after we left Nero's. It might just be damage to the camera unit, but I want a third opinion. *Adios, amiga.*"

"*Hasta luego,*" Abby replied. *Yeah, see you later when we have more privileged information we want to feed Winifred.*

***

"Well, that was enlightening," Winifred said after Abby and Arlie had gone in different directions. "Intentional or otherwise, Arlie, thanks for sharing."

She looked down at the deskpad notes she'd taken and her initial questions.

Why Y at bakery?

Why L and kid know Y?

Why L talk funny?

She crossed off the last one and added another to the list:

Why Y still around?

"It's obvious that Louie knows Yakov. Since he's also in Witness Protection, I'd say he knows Yakov from his previous life. But what's the deal with Arlie's kid? And why is he so sharp? He must have had

169

a rough early life.

"Hmm. Arlie, single forever and suddenly married with two kids. Just by looking, I can tell the boys are his. Since their birthdays are a few days apart, they can't be twins. That means two mothers. Foxy Arlie. And here I thought you were boring that way."

***

Louie scanned the back of the envelope with the list of potential caterers he and Jess had drawn up. "Hey, Northern Lights Delights Bakery in Wasilla isn't on this. I know Donna and Paul bake the best apple fritters on Alaska – shoot, maybe in the world – but maybe she caters, too. Can I call and find out?"

"Of course, you can," Jess said. "You don't have to ask my permission." He picked up one more bacon and cheese twist, started to put it back on the platter, then changed his mind and ate it. "Just make sure you don't order another sampler for a day or two. These finger foods are fantastic, but I'm going to be as big as a moose if I keep eating like this. Salads and veggies for the next two days, all right?"

"Yeah, well, maybe," Louie teased. "I'd love you no matter how skinny or fat you got. As long as you're healthy, that's all that matters to me."

"Me, too." Jess looked at his watch. "Hey, I'd better get back to work. Coming home for lunch is better than fast food."

"Hey, this is fast food. You drove up and I had your order ready to eat: leftovers."

"True." Jess gave Louie a quick hug and a kiss. "I have just enough time to pop in and give LuLu a kiss goodbye."

"Nope," Louie said, shaking his head. "It's her naptime. Rita won't let you disturb her, even for a quick peck on the forehead. I can hear her now, 'You'll have to wait until you come home tonight. She has to keep to a routine, or she'll be cranky for the rest of the day.'"

"Yeah," Jess agreed. "By the way, Tina's coming back from her assignment this afternoon. Maybe they'd like to share some of these *hors d'oeuvres.* Just a thought. Your decision. Love ya! Bye."

Talking about LuLu had given Louie that antsy, empty-arms feeling again. He used the extra energy to clean up the already clean kitchen. Just as he was getting ready to vacuum the living room for the second time in one day, he saw his list of potential caterers.

"It's early enough that she should still be there." Louie scrolled through the contacts on his phone and found Donna's number.

"Hey, Donna. This is Louie, your adopted son. Well, kind of adopted. I was pretty sure you knew me. But anyhow, I didn't even think to ask you, but since Jess and I are getting married sometime in the not-too-distant future, I wanted to know if you cater special events. Oh, not too soon. No sooner than three weeks, but most likely a few months. So, do you cater weddings? Well, if you're still considering it as a side business, could you maybe put together a list of finger foods available? No, I don't think we need mini-fritters, at least for the wedding. Oh, that's right – the wedding cake. We'll have you make the cake, even if you don't cater.

"Oh, I'm sorry. I didn't even ask how you were. I know Charlene said you had some jerk of a customer come in and stick you with a

171

couple of bogus hundred-dollar bills. Yeah, Yakov's a real creep.

"How'd I know his name? Well, you know how Arlie's an undercover detective and all. Well, he didn't even have to be undercover to figure that one out.

"Wait. What? He called you? Are you sure it was Yakov? I mean, are you sure it was the guy who almost hit Charlene's car? Are you kidding me? He was asking if you had Mount Spurr Sourdough in stock? He called it what? Nero's sourdough that came in a paper bag with the picture of a steaming volcano on it... Yeah, that's Mount Spurr, alright.

"Did he give you a phone number? Oh, that'll work. I'll wait. I'm sure glad phones have caller ID. What did folks do in the old days? Oh, okay. I've got a pen. Got it. That's sure a lot of sevens. It must be a burn phone. Makes sense since he's such a creep.

"Oh, and I'll check your website for what goodies you offer. I'll make up a list and send you an order for a sampler. And for the wedding cake, we'll probably just go with your awesome carrot cake. That and a lot of little apple fritters. Man, I just ate and now I'm hungry all over again talking about cakes and fritters. Okay. I'll let you know if I find out anything about Yakov. Yeah, Yucky Yakov, is right. He's hard to forget."

Louie looked at the phone number. Should he bother Arlie with this new information? Yakov looking for a certain kind of sourdough bread was kind of boring. "Nah. It can wait until he gets home from work. Four hours won't make that much difference."

Knock. Knock.

Louie answered the back door. "Hey, Char. Come on in. If you're hungry, I have lots and lots of 'horse divorces' leftover. Or like Carlos says, maybe I should just call them finger foods. I can't seem to get the French accent right."

Charlene shook her head. "None for me. I already ate lunch. I just came over to give this back." She handed him a big brown paper bag, the top folded over like it was a giant lunch sack.

Louie opened it and looked inside. "Gee, thanks!"

"I know it's your favorite hat. Abby said you left it at her office earlier. She gave it to Arlie to give to you. He came home a few minutes ago, on his way to wherever. I can't keep up with him, and he asked me not to try. That was an easy one to say yes to."

"Cool!" Louie took it out of the bag and put it on. "Yeah, it's my favorite ballcap. Hey, when Arlie calls in next time, I have a phone number for him. Oh, and I have some strange information to give him about that guy, Yakov. It might mean something to him but not to me."

Louie adjusted his cap and continued. "I guess Yakov called Donna at her bakery in Wasilla a little while ago. He asked her if she had any Nero's sourdough bread. She didn't know what he was talking about until he said it was in a bag with a picture of a smoking volcano on it. Mount Spurr Sourdough is the brand name of the stuff Nero baked. Nero's the guy who was just murdered. That's the case Jess and I are helping Arlie solve. Well, Abby and Winifred are kind of working on it, too. And maybe some more people, I don't know. I wouldn't know because I'm not on the force or with the FBI. Well, except I'm with Jess, and he's with the FBI…"

Charlene put her hand on Louie's shoulder, stopping his blathering. "You're bored and miss LuLu when she's with her mother, don't you?"

"Oh, man, I sure do. My little girl's growing up so fast. I want another baby. I think Jess does, too. But, well, you know…"

Charlene shook her head, remembering the hassle Louie and Rita went through, adapting to shared parenting for LuLu. "I just popped over to give you the baseball cap. I have to get back home. Harlie Jae's napping."

"Yeah, so's LuLu. Remember the old days when you thought they'd never go to sleep? Now you want them to hurry and wake up so you can hang out with them."

"You're right, Louie. I think you need another baby – or at least another project – in your life." She gave him a quick hug. "I'm sure you'll find an outlet for that extra energy somewhere. Have faith. I do."

Louie watched as Charlene rushed across his backyard and through the back gate to her home. "Well, one of us having faith is better than none of us."

CHAPTER 15: A FRIENDLY FAVOR
OR A DANGEROUS SETUP

Crackle. Crackle

"Ah, his cap is coming back out of the bag. What golden nuggets of information do you have for me today, Louie?"

Winifred minimized the image of the report she'd been studying on her computer, the one she'd screen-captured from the feed from Louie's 'fly on the file cabinet' baseball cap when it was in Abby's office earlier.

If she didn't know better – and she didn't – she'd swear Arlie had strategically positioned himself and the laptop and was feeding her information. Well, if he was, thank you. If not, what kind of sloppy cop are you, Arlie Biggar?

"Let there be light," Winifred whispered as Louie's ball cap came back into action. She adjusted her earpiece and shut her eyes to concentrate on what Louie was telling Charlene.

Winifred jotted notes on her deskpad, marking down keywords.

Phone number

Strange information

Yakov

Her eyes opened wide at the name. She pulled out the earbuds, turned up the volume, and scribbled another remark.

Nero's sourdough – Mount Spurr

Winifred listened anxiously as Louie babbled about helping solve the case with the others, then something about wanting more babies.

Two blinks later, Winifred zoned out, lost in her own world of loss and remorse. She realized what she'd done and looked up. The screen was dark again. She rewound the video and saw Louie had put the cap back in the bag.

"Damn!"

Three times she watched and listened to the recording, but she kept coming to the same conclusion. Yakov wanted some of Nero's sourdough.

But why?

Bzzz. Bzzz.

Winifred looked at the caller ID.

Louie.

"Hello, Louie," she said brightly. "How are you this beautiful day?"

"Oh, me? I'm fine. Hey, I was wondering, since you and Nero were friends, did you ever eat any of his sourdough bread? I think they called it Mount Spurr Sourdough."

"Yes… As a matter of fact, I did. I have about ten loaves of it in my freezer now. Why?"

"Um, I kinda sort of have a special request for some of it. I could lie to you and tell you I just wanted to see if it was as good as everyone says, but I know you. You'd see right through me."

"Louie, one of your great liabilities is also your greatest asset: you can't lie worth a darn. Yes, you can come over and have a loaf of it. No questions asked. But I want you to do me one favor, maybe

177

two."

"Okay."

"Would you wear that ball cap I gave you? I want to show community spirit for our local baseball club. You're pretty much a walking billboard when you have it on."

"So, what's the second favor?"

Winifred chuckled. "I'm not sure yet, but I'm sure I'll need something."

"Okay. See you soon."

Louie reached up and grabbed the keys to the Jeep. Just as he opened the front door, he remembered it.

"Gotta wear the hat." He reached into the top of the closet and grabbed the bag it was in. "Go Chinooks!" he said and settled the cap on his head.

Fifteen minutes later, he was at Winifred's front door. He heard it unlock and turned the handle. "Anyone home?"

"I'm over here," Winifred said, the remote for the lock to her secure front door in hand. "I think you and I need to talk."

"Is that your second favor?" he asked, pulling a kitchen chair next to her.

"No. Talking isn't a favor."

"Yeah, but revealing secrets is. What do you want to know, Winifred?"

"Everything you know."

"Oh, man. That will take forever..."

"Not your life history, Louie. Your call earlier this afternoon.

You know, the sourdough bread? Why do you want it?"

"Um, someone else does. I was hoping to get some information out of him. It's bait for Yakov. I…" Louie stood up anxiously and put his cap on top of her monitor. A small squelch of feedback came from the computer's speaker.

Winifred reached over and turned the volume all the way down.

"Hey," Louie said and took the hat back. He looked down at it, then held it close to his chest. "This is a spy hat like Jess's See-Hawks ball cap, isn't it?"

"Yes. Is there a problem with that?"

"You're darned tootin' there is. When you're watching people and listening to everything they do or say, you're supposed to let them know."

"No, you're not," Winifred replied coolly. "When you walk down the street or," she looked up at the hat, "go to a ballgame, you don't go up to every person and ask permission to see or listen to whatever's going on around them. That's simply impossible to do."

"Yeah, well…well… You can watch and listen, but you can't record them. I'll bet dollars to donuts that you have everything I've said or done while wearing this hat recorded somewhere on that computer."

"Which do you want?"

"Huh?"

"Dollars or donuts."

Louie huffed and sat down. "Sourdough bread. Here's what's going on. Maybe you can help me."

In his convoluted way, Louie explained what he wanted to do: entrap Yakov into confessing. He held up his smartphone. "I'll have it set to record before I go in. That should work, huh?"

Winifred shrugged. "It would be better if you went in wearing a tank top and track shorts so Yakov can see that you don't have a wire. If he feels uncomfortable, he'll ask you to leave your phone outside, put it in a Faraday bag, or the refrigerator."

"Huh?"

"Conversations are a little hard to record when the phone signals are blocked by shielding from a refrigerator or a Faraday bag. But let's keep it simple. Wear your track clothes and ball cap. He'll see how much skin you're revealing and won't ask for a scan or pat down. I'll give you a loaf of my bread and some special dipping sauce."

"Like fry sauce or ranch dressing?" Louie asked.

"Nope. Yakov doesn't have American tastes. Balsamic vinegar is more his style. I'll mix some up for you to take to him. Don't you eat any of it, though"

"Why? Is it poisonous or something?"

"Nope. It'll have so much grain alcohol in it, he should be as chatty as if he'd had a fifth of Russian vodka. He'll answer any questions you ask. Or brag about his latest accomplishments. Most likely, he'll talk about food and conquests. Since he still hasn't come out of the closet, he won't talk about his love life. Or lack of it. Steer the conversation away from foods. He'll never shut up about that."

"But why does he want the bread?" Louie asked.

"My guess is that he's trying to duplicate Nero's recipe. He's either found another source or he's baked some himself. He wants to see if they taste the same."

"Hey, if I take some of my own dip or garlic butter, we can break and compare breads together. Guys like bonding over food and conquests that are similar. I guess I can make up something tough since I never killed anyone. Or hurt anyone. Not on purpose, anyhow."

"No."

"Huh? I thought you wanted me to…"

"Louie, you're a lousy liar. Don't even try. He'll suspect something if you do. Oh, and don't drink or eat anything other than what you bring with you. Just because you're not poisoning him doesn't mean he won't off you if he suspects you're tricking him. Which you are."

"Okay. And let's hope he doesn't recognize me. Maybe I should use my southern accent."

"Absolutely not. And recognize you? From where, Louie? No, never mind. I don't need to know. Just get him to talk about himself. Don't talk about you. If you hear yourself say 'I,' immediately stammer and change the subject to something about him. Can you do that?"

"I guess. Is that your second favor, Winifred?"

"Yes, I suppose it is. Give him a call and tell him you have the bread. Set up a meeting for an hour from now. It can be wherever he wants. But when you get there, make sure you have at least two exits, both from the house or motel where he is, and from the neighborhood. And keep your baseball cap on all the time. If you have to, say you had a bad haircut and want to keep it covered."

"But you said I'm a lousy liar."

Winifred reached up and quickly cut a lock of hair off the top of Louie's head. "Problem solved."

"Hey! That's not nice," he said, rubbing his hand over the stubble at his crown.

"Maybe not, but if it saves your life, you'll thank me. Now, hang tight. I have to get your food basket put together. Hmm. Maybe two loaves and two quarts of dip would be better. With his bulk and drinking experience, he probably has a high tolerance to any kind of alcohol. Go ahead and look in my refrigerator for whatever spreads or sauces you want for the bread you eat. I doubt you'll have time to go shopping."

"This is getting more complicated than I thought." Louie rubbed his little reverse Mohawk haircut. "So much for having nice hair for my wedding pictures."

***

"There. You're set. I put the bread in the microwave for a few minutes to defrost. I don't want to cook it or dry it out, but it was as hard as granite. It should be pretty much thawed by the time you get there. Where's the hook-up spot?"

"You already listened in on my call and know it's a forty-minute drive from here." Louie took the bag of bread and dip from her and dropped in a tub of soft butter. "Remind me again why I'm doing this?"

Winifred paled. It may have been Louie's idea, but she should be talking him out of it, not pushing him toward a dangerous situation. He had no formal training or backup. Getting Yakov to confess wasn't his job, and it wasn't hers either.

Louie answered his own question. "Oh, yeah. Because I'm the one who found out Yakov was looking for Nero's sourdough."

"Yes, and the evidence Abby and Arlie collected isn't enough to convict anyone. No murder weapon, so no fingerprints."

"Geez, it almost sounds like the perfect murder. Let's see if I still have all that luck that got me the nickname of Lucky."

Winifred picked up the Chinooks cap from the kitchen table. "And remember to wear this at all times."

"Yes, ma'am. I'll get a confession and be back in time for supper."

***

"Damn! Damn! Damn!"

"Arlie Biggar, what's gotten into you?" Charlene said, her hands over Harlie Jae's ears.

"Damn, damn, damn," the toddler repeated, then giggled.

"I'm sorry, Charlene." He gave her a quick kiss, then rushed into the hall closet and grabbed his 'to go' bag.

"Uh-oh. That bad?" she asked, ignoring her daughter's new word. She watched wordlessly as he kitted up with Kevlar, adding a loose-fitting flannel shirt to disguise it.

It was bad news when Arlie swore.

It was even worse when he didn't talk.

Charlene remained mum, bouncing the baby in her arms, giving Harlie Jae quick affectionate squeezes for her own reassurance.

Once he was done with his routine of arming and protecting himself for an emergency undercover operation, Arlie spoke.

"Winifred and Louie are cooking up some half-baked scheme to get Yakov to admit to murdering Nero."

"What?" Charlene screeched. The toddler started to cry but was quickly soothed by mommy kisses. "Now I know why you said... Well, what you said."

"Damn, damn, damn!" Harlie Jae crowed.

"That's dang, dang, dang," Arlie told her. "I said it wrong the first time."

"Dang, dang, dang," Harlie repeated.

Chip and Carlos came running in from the backyard. "Mom, can we turn on the hose and wash the car again?"

"No, but you can go in the kitchen and wash some grapes. And take your sister with you and share them with her. Don't let her have more than one at a time. And that goes for you and your brother, too. Chew each grape completely before putting another one in your mouth or you won't get them again for a year!"

"Geez, why's Mom so cranky?" Chip asked as the three of them walked into the kitchen.

Carlos looked back at their parents. His father looked bulkier. Yes, he was wearing his bullet-proof vest and probably had an extra gun or two tucked in his clothes somewhere. Dad was going someplace dangerous, and Mom was scared.

"Maybe she has a headache. Let's go wash the grapes, then we can have a tea party with Harlie. We can eat real food this time and let her be the waitress."

"I want to be the waitress," Chip said.

"Okay, but I think it's called a waiter or a cook or something else when it's a guy. Waitresses are women."

"As long as I get to take everyone's order and bring the food, I don't care."

***

Arlie watched his children leave the room. Chip and Harlie Jae were oblivious to what was going on. But not Carlos.

"I don't know if I told you or not," Arlie said to Charlene, "But Louie told me that Yakov was one of the hitmen Papa De Luca sent after Carlos. The poor boy was only about four years old at the time. Louie said he'd run interference without either side knowing what he was doing. He'd pinch Carlos or something else to make him scream, alerting his mother that something was wrong, and spoiling the hit. Rosa did her best to keep her son safe from her husband's jealousy." Arlie shook his head. "But I don't think Carlos would have made it as long as he did without Louie intentionally gumming up the works for Papa's hitmen."

"So, what are you going to do now? No, scratch that. I don't really want to know. I'm sure you'll do the right thing. Oh, I did tell you Louie had some information, didn't I?"

"Um, no…"

"Shit! I mean, shoot. Call Donna at the bakery. When Louie talked to her, she said Yakov had called there, looking for some of Nero's sourdough bread."

Arlie nodded. "Yeah, I got that when I hacked into the feed from Louie's hat. I got the phone number from Donna, too. The tracker's still on Yakov's car, so I know where I'm going. By the time I'm on the road, I'll have back up everywhere."

Or should.

***

"Abby, is Buzz still with you?"

"Of course, she is, Arlie. You and I are the only ones authorized to use her."

"And that authorization only comes from us since it's our private property. Damn. I need her out in Wasilla stat. I don't have time to drive to Anchorage, pick her up, and get back to..."

"To where?" Abby prompted.

"Never mind. Let me make a call. I might have a second-string player who's closer. Oh, and whatever you do, don't let Winifred know what I'm up to. She's not thinking right, or she wouldn't have sent Louie into a dangerous situation. Besides, I gave her plenty of clues that I knew how to hack into Louie's cap, but she seemed oblivious."

"Yeah, I could tell when we were at the site earlier that she was mighty fond of Nero."

"Yup, and her grief has clouded her judgment big time. Sending Louie on a half-baked venture that even I wouldn't go on... Damn! If

Louie gets hurt."

"Arlie, don't let your feelings for him cloud your judgment, too," Abby said.

"You're right. Sorry. So, if she gets a recording of Yakov confessing to the murder, great. Right now, all I care about is getting Louie away from Yakov in one living, breathing, loveable piece."

"Agreed. If you need…"

"Hey," Arlie cut her off. "I gotta make a call. Here's hoping Eddie is somewhere close and has her pet drone with her."

"Bye."

Click.

Tap, tap.

"Hey, Eddie. Okay, I'll hold." Arlie paced in circles. Even if he had tried to tell her, Eddie couldn't have heard him say, 'Hurry up. This is urgent.' Road and motorcycle noises swallowed up any conversation. Her heads-up display showed him on the caller ID. She'd call back ASAP.

Ten seconds later, she said, "Shoot."

"Louie's in trouble in Wasilla. How close are you and do you have your drone with you?"

"Half hour or less away, and Eddie III is always with me."

"I thought it was Eddie II."

"I made a few modifications to a smaller unit. Eddie III is the same size as Buzz. I never did get around to adding a voice chip, but I do have some other useful noises I can call up if needed."

"Louie's in room 112 at the Night and Day Inn. Nero's murderer,

Yakov, is there with him. Oh, and those two have a history. Here's hoping Yakov doesn't remember him as Lucky. If he does, Louie's luck may run out."

"Bad blood?" Eddie asked as she verified the battery was still charged on her camouflaged drone.

"You don't rob a hit man of a kill and make him your friend. Do you still have the low battery alert on the drone, and can you override it, giving it a voice?"

"Yes and yes, and I already have. One for yes, two for no, and three for get the hell out of there?"

"When it's safe, give Louie three chirps. Here's hoping he knows what it means."

"And Plan B?" Eddie asked.

"That is Plan B. I'm going in as Plan A."

CHAPTER 16: IS LOUIE LUCKY OR DOOMED?

Wasilla, 40 minutes later

Louie pulled up to the address Yakov had given him, a two-story hotel at the edge of town. Before he parked, he did as Winifred said and made sure there were at least two ways to leave. That was easy since the hotel was on the Parks Highway, the main road in the area. Even if both exits were blocked, he could still make it onto the thoroughfare. The ground was mostly flat and dry, and he was in the Jeep. An off-roading exit strategy would be easy to pull off if needed.

He looked at his note with the room number, and then at the building. Cool. Yakov was on the first floor. He could jump out a window if Yakov blocked the door. Two exits from the room, too.

Louie saw and recognized Yakov even before he turned off the engine. He didn't pay any attention to him because he wasn't supposed to know what he looked like. Instead, he poked around in the shopping bag on the passenger seat next to him.

"Are you man with Nero's sourdough bread?" Yakov called out when Louie got out of the Jeep.

Louie hoisted the paper grocery sack with the two loaves of bread and jars of Winifred's secret sauce. "That's me. I guess you're the guy I'm looking for."

Yakov frowned as he looked Louie up and down, studying the wiry frame and casual attire. This was a boy, and a skinny one at that.

190

He could not be a baker. He must only be a courier. Bakers were always fat because they ate their own food. Still, in a pinch, this one would do. He had both hands, could walk, and see well enough to drive delivery trucks. He would do as the first man to work in his bakery.

Uncomfortable at being checked out like he was a piece of art to be purchased, Louie started to ask if there was a problem. Instead, he took a deep breath and did as Winifred said: wait and let Yakov do all the talking. *He needs to believe he's in charge of the situation.*

"Why you standing outside all day, almost naked boy?" Yakov asked and waved for him to follow. "Come inside and we talk before you freeze to death."

Louie blushed crimson. He was both embarrassed about being called naked and enraged at being called a boy. *Shut up. Shut up. Shut up! Don't respond to his taunts. He's a crazy murderer who enjoys making his victims mad. Stay cool. Just get his confession, then hightail it out of here. Winifred will take it from there.*

Yakov pushed the door open, kicking away the ice bucket he'd used as a door stop. "Come in. I want you tell me which bread taste good like Nero's sourdough."

The standard four-foot round motel room table was near the window, curtains pulled halfway back, sunlight playing on the colorful assortment of various shapes and colors of bagged bread, a treasure trove of sourdough varieties.

"How…how many do I have to sample?" Louie asked, nodding to the Jenga pile, precariously tilting to one side.

"Enough or all," Yakov grunted. "You stay until we find right one to help me decide."

How is this going to get me a confession? Think, Louie, think!

Yakov set out two big plates and a bottle of vodka, motioning for him to sit down.

Louie sat and looked closer at the dull finish on the plates. It appeared as if someone had licked them clean and missed a few spots. *Don't deny him what he wants, or you'll be in even more trouble.*

"Um, I can help with the taste test, but I can't drink alcohol. I have a medical condition. I take pills for," Louie swallowed hard, trying to think of a disease that would have a bad reaction to liquor. He feigned a cough. "Excuse me. I have to take pills for diabetes. I really wish I could drink, but the doctor said I'd probably die if I did. You don't want to have a dead body in your room, do you?"

Yakov shrugged as if it was only a minor inconvenience. "Okay. You drink faucet water if you get thirsty. Here, I get started with Nero's sourdough bread first." He pulled a long knife out from behind him. "I cut good. Very good."

Louie watched as Yakov sliced off a thick slab of Nero's Mount Spurr Sourdough bread. "Not too much for me," Louie said. "I had a big lunch before I came here. I didn't know we were going to eat."

"No worries. You take bite of Nero's bread first, then bite of one other bread. You give it either..." Yakov grinned broadly, showing two rotten front teeth. He gave a thumbs-up gesture with one hand. "Or..." Yakov scowled, bushy salt-and-pepper eyebrows crowding together as he drew his commando-style knife in front of his throat.

"We kill it. Tossing it into bonfire."

Yakov watched Louie's eyes widen in shock. He chuckled at the fear he'd caused. "Or we just throw it in trash and get more bread."

"Oh, yeah. I like that idea better. I'm not sure if you can have a bonfire – or any other kind of fire – right now. They've had a lot of trouble with wildfires around here lately."

Wildfires? Why didn't you steer the topic over to knives? It was right there, dude.

Louie glanced up at the sound of liquid pouring. Yakov was pouring vodka into a glass.

"You sure you not want just a little vodka?" he asked. "Maybe it not kill you this time."

"Nah," Louie said. "I'm not feeling too lucky today."

At the word 'lucky,' Yakov raised one eyebrow as if he'd just remembered something. He looked closer at Louie.

Why in the hell did you use the word lucky? Now he's thinking of that other skinny dude from his past, the one who wouldn't drink with the guys. You! Lucky De Luca. Crap! Think fast. Change the subject!

"Oh, yeah," Louie said. He stood up and ruffled through the paper sack. "I just remembered something: this." He held up a quart jar of balsamic vinegar blended with grain alcohol. "It's really good for dunking your bread in, the lady said."

"What lady?" Yakov asked, the same eyebrow popped up again in suspicion.

"Oh, there's this little old lady who lives near me. Well, kind of near me," Louie said, making sure he didn't lie. "She keeps extra stuff in her freezer for me. I had to get the bread from her. She said I should try this balsamic vinegar dip with it. She insisted it made great bread taste even better. Just that much sweeter." Louie pinched his thumb and forefinger almost together in illustration.

"Well, I didn't want to tell her I couldn't have it if it was sweet, so I brought it along for you. I figured you might want to try it. She wouldn't have given it to me if it was bad. If you like it, the next time I see her, I can tell her it..." Louie held up thumb and forefinger again. "Made bread just that much sweeter and a great sourdough taste even greater."

Yakov frowned, his bottom lip stuck out like a child trying to figure out if he wanted to throw a temper tantrum or not. He shrugged. "Okay. I like sweet."

Louie unscrewed the cap on the one-quart canning jar and set it aside. "I guess you can dip it right into the jar." He held it up to his nose, sniffed, and exclaimed truthfully. "Man, this stuff smells great!"

"You try first," Yakov said.

"Well, okay," Louie said, reading doubt on Yakov's face. "I guess just a tiny bit won't kill me. At least, I hope not."

Louie dipped his pinkie in the dark brown liquid and tasted it. "Oh, man. I wish I could have more. This is so good, I could drink it straight."

"Go ahead," Yakov prompted.

"Nah. I don't want to leave my daughter an orphan. Nothing tastes that good." He pushed the jar away from him, then picked it up and sniffed it again. "But if I didn't have a kid, I'd be tempted."

194

Yakov picked up the jar and took a sip. This time, both eyebrows went up and so did his mustache. "Da. Very good!"

He tore off a piece of the bread he'd just sliced, then dunked it, offering it to Louie. "You sure, skinny boy?"

Louie's tongue was cool, almost numb. If he was tempted by its great taste – and he was – the chill was a reminder. *Remember, Winifred said, 'Don't drink any of it.'*

"Yeah, I'm sure. Hey, do you want me to slice some of this other bread, or do you want to do all the cutting? We have a lot to compare before it's time for me to go." Louie looked at his fitness tracker watch. "I told the sitter I wouldn't be gone too long."

"Hmph!" Yakov crossed his arms in front of him and stared at Louie, his face devoid of any emotion other than uncertainty. "Not what I had planned."

Louie ignored the comment and instead, took the lead. Standing up again, he took two loaves of bread from the pile. "How about these two? They're not from the big bakeries, so might taste as good. Or at least, they won't taste like that gummy cardboard the mega stores put out."

Yakov took the two loaves and looked at them. "Yes, big bakeries use electric, not wood, for their ovens. Make bread taste bad."

He shoved one loaf back to Louie and slit the wrapper from the other one. "This label say wood-fired oven. Maybe it taste great, too." He quickly sliced off two pieces and handed one to Louie. "You check first."

"Sure." Louie took a bite, chewed thoughtfully, then spat it into the trash.

"Why you do that?"

Louie picked up the piece of Nero's sourdough and took a bite of it. This time, he shut his eyes as he chewed, savoring the nuances. "Close but not the same. Still, it's good, so let's put this loaf aside. We can check it later, after we've checked the other ones."

"I ask you, why you spit out?"

"Oh, I thought that's what you were supposed to do. I know that's what they do at wine tastings. Not that I've ever been to one, but that's what they do on those TV shows. Disgusting, huh?"

"Who would spit out good wine?"

Louie shrugged. "I don't know. The reason I spat mine out was so I'd have room to taste or eat more. Go ahead and try this one. Oh, and you might want to try it with the dip, too."

"Why you want me to eat dip?"

Louie rolled his eyes, trying to think of a plausible explanation. "Because the bread could taste different without the dip. That's what I'm doing: tasting these naked. When you try them, you can see if these and Nero's taste the same with the balsamic sauce...or whatever it's called. I think that's a double-blind test. If not, we can call it a dip and un-dip test."

Yakov looked skeptical but stayed mum. Again.

Louie started to break out in a sweat. *You didn't do anything wrong. He's baiting you. Silence is meant to intimidate. Don't let him see you get nervous.*

"Is it hot in here?" Louie asked. He stood up without waiting for an answer. "Do you mind if I open this window a little? It might only be in the low seventies, but it must be extra humid today. Man, how do people live in hot countries?"

Louie pulled the curtain all the way open to find the latch for the windows.

Buzz.

Hovering just outside the window was Arlie and Abby's smart drone. Louie only noticed Buzz because he had seen her elevate rapidly, trying to get out of sight.

"What? You not know how to open window?"

"Oh, I guess I was waiting for you to say it was okay. I am your guest and all. Sometimes I get a little pushy. I just really, really don't like to get too hot."

"Maybe it because of diabetes," Yakov said, studying Louie's unease.

"Diabetes?" Louie faltered. "Huh? Oh, no. I don't think that has anything to do with it. I think it's because I'm a redhead. We don't do so well in the sun. I guess that's why I live in Alaska. We get lots of sun in the summer, but it's not a hot sun." Louie wiped his sweaty brow. "Or at least, most of the time it isn't."

Louie turned around and looked for the window latch again, this time ignoring everything else. He had his task to do. If Buzz was here, so was Arlie. They would have to work around him. He got to Yakov first. "There! Got it."

Yakov inhaled deeply, loudly.

Louie looked back at him, and then at the empty tumbler. The man's cheeks were flushed. He was unsteady on his feet.

And the bottle of vodka was half-empty.

"Drinking from glass too much trouble. Bottle faster. Besides, I have better use for glass."

Yakov poured the remaining balsamic dip into the tumbler and drank it down with four hearty glug-glugs. "Good enough to drink straight. You ask old lady for more." He stifled a burp. "Good. Very good, even without bread."

"Aren't we going to test more of these?" Louie pointed to the breads, now spread out.

"Why? You said this one good."

"Well, yes. I just thought you wanted to try more of them," Louie said, backing away as Yakov approached him.

Now just inches away, Yakov bent towards Louie and sniffed his neck. "You smell like fear. Are you afraid of me?"

Louie stepped back and composed himself. "You? Why should I be afraid of you? No, I'm not afraid of you, but I am a little concerned about a man who's drunk a half quart of vodka and suddenly changes his mind about why he called me."

"Smart boy. Quick thinker. You should be afraid of me." Yakov uncapped the other jar of balsamic dip and took a long gulp. He set it back on the table, sloshing some of the contents as he set it down, his loss of motor control obvious to both of them.

"Yes, you should be afraid of me. I kill people. Sometimes for money. Sometimes for fun." Yakov's eyes started to tear up.

"Sometimes for…well, you know."

"Sometimes for love?" Louie asked.

Yakov looked Louie up and down, pouting again as if he was deciding whether he was the flavor of ice cream he wanted or not. "How would you know? You have wife and kid. You do not know what wrong love is."

Shut up, Louie. Don't volunteer anything. Remember, do not say anything with the word I in it. He wouldn't understand if you told him, 'I don't have a wife. I'm gay.' You're not here to make him your friend or help him come out of the closet. You're here to get him to confess to murder.

"You're right. I don't understand. So, how about we check out all the small store breads first?" Louie moved toward the pile and was blocked by Yakov stepping in front of him. "Excuse me," Louie said.

"I just tell you I kill people and you not care?" Yakov asked, his eyes red-rimmed and his stance wavering.

"Nope," Louie answered honestly. "I'm not a cop and you don't know me. I just came here to bring you a couple of loaves of bread from my private stash. By the way…" Louie pulled on his chin where a goatee would be if he had one. "Didn't you say something about paying top money for this bread? Maybe I should have asked for it before letting you eat any." *Good. Show no fear. Get back to the facts as he knows them.*

"Da." Yakov reached in his front pocket and pulled two hundred-dollar bills off his roll. He paused, then peeled off two more. "Two for bread and two for brown juicy dip. You tell your lady friend I buy all blas…balls… I buy all brown vinegar dip she make. To hell with bread. This will make even bad bread taste good."

"So, you're not trying to bake bread like Nero's?" Louie asked.

"Yes and no. It is good bread but other breads good, too. I find out having my own bakery too much trouble. Plan to put other bread in my own packaging is too much trouble, too. It better to sell dip that make any bread taste great. Lady friend's sweet brown juice is better business opportunity. I make lots of money selling it instead."

Louie nodded to the pocket Yakov had pulled the wad of cash from. "It doesn't look like you're hurting for money."

Yakov shrugged. "When I run out, I can always get more. So, you work for me and sell sweet brown juice?"

Louie shook his head and frowned. "Nope. I have a full-time job." *Damn! There's that word I!*

Yakov picked up his knife and gently brushed breadcrumbs from it, looking up at Louie with a menacing smile. "You forget I kill people?"

"Why would you want to kill me? If you did, you wouldn't know where to get 'sweet brown juice,'" Louie said, using Yakov's Russian accent at the end.

Yakov looked down at the crotch of Louie's track shorts. "You have big balls, skinny man."

Louie reached down and covered his private parts, then brought his hand back up to his face. "Eyes up here, dude. Big balls or no balls, I'm the only one who knows where to get 'sweet brown juice.' And how do I know you're not lying about killing people? I haven't

200

heard anything on the news about anyone being killed in…in…ages."

"I didn't say when I kill people," Yakov said, wavering even more. "Or where." He picked up the jar of balsamic drink and savored another sip. "Ah. Yes, I kill man just yesterday. Close by. In Anchorage. Perfect murder. No weapon."

"So, people die all the time without weapons. Car crashes, heart attacks, strokes, cancer."

Yakov stepped up to Louie, the quart jar with the last two inches of brown brew held close to his heart, like a child clutching his teddy bear. "I kill Nero who bakes great sourdough bread and it not on the news?"

Yakov held an index finger in front of his bushy black mustache, deep in thought. "That because Nero really man name Sonny who is Witness Protection. No one want to talk about it. People sneak in to take away body. Very hush hush."

"So, Nero had a heart attack. It happens all the time."

"Witness Protection. Hush. *Belch.* Hush."

Louie backed away at the stink, but Yakov came closer still. He bent to Louie's neck, sniffing again. "Just little bit of fear. You know death. You not afraid as most people. You in Witness Protection, too?"

"I watched my mother die," Louie said, fire in his eyes. "She was murdered. The murderer got away with it."

"Maybe I murder your mother. Lucky."

Louie was so pissed at recalling his mother's death that he didn't realize he had just been baited again. "Lucky my mother died? No, that wasn't lucky for anyone."

Yakov frowned. "No, I kill mother of man named Lucky. It was only lucky for me I not caught. I sell knife to pawn shop cheap and hope it gone quick. I much smarter now. I use frozen icicle. Hard, sharp, and it disappear…"

Yakov put his free hand in the air, opening it quickly like a burst of fireworks. "It disappear. No weapon found. No fingerprints. Nothing. Perfect murder."

Louie focused on the jar Yakov was holding close to his chest, burying his negative emotions in the brown sloshing liquid so, Yakov couldn't read him. "No witnesses, either?" he asked without looking away. "Yeah, I guess that makes it a perfect murder."

Screech! Screech!

A loud call came from outside the window, distracting them at the perfect time.

"What is that?" Yakov asked, looking around, confused.

Louie took the opportunity to escape his penned-in position. He squatted down, passed under the Yakov' elbow, and dashed to the window, making certain he couldn't be cornered again.

The noise came from the drone but not the one he thought he'd seen earlier. This one was smaller and camouflage colored.

"Where…where eagle?" Yakov slurred. He reached out with his jar-free arm and steadied himself against the wall.

"I…I don't see it," Louie said shakily.

He could hear himself lying, so knew Yakov could, too. "If it was an eagle, it's gone now," he added with conviction. "Don't worry.

Eagles are all over the place around here. I'm sure you'll see one later. The river's just down there."

"Oh?" Yakov cozied up to Louie and looked out the window. "You mean eagles eat fishes?"

"Yeah." Louie glanced to his side, making sure he wouldn't trip on anything when it was time to run out of there. "But they prefer to eat guts and other spoils left behind by fisherman. They're really lazy. They'd rather eat leftovers than hunt."

"Noo…" Yakov said, inching closer to Louie. He licked his bottom lip, lust in his eyes.

"Yeah, it's true." Louie took just one small step away, adjusting his position in front of the window, so it didn't look like he was scared or running.

"You mean eagle is opportunist? Any food when hungry."

"Yeah, something like that."

"Well, I opportunist, too. I hungry. But not for food." Yakov leaned forward to sniff Louie's neck, but Louie had seen the leer. He was ready to bolt when a new sound came from outside.

Chirp. Chirp. Chirp.

"What? What…? Yakov babbled.

But Louie didn't answer him. He was already gone.

Louie didn't know what the code meant but did know it was electronic and probably came from the drone. Whether it was a friend, foe, or a stranger flying the device, Louie was making use of Yakov's distraction to scram.

"Where you go, skinny boy?" Yakov called out after him.

"Oh, he had a prior commitment," Arlie said, stepping in front of the motel room door Louie had left open.

Yakov reached behind his back and grabbed for his knife.

But it was gone.

He looked at the table with the pushed-up pile of sourdough breads, the knife sitting in front of them.

"Not so fast," Arlie said, smacking his version of a slap bracelet on the confused man's right hand.

Yakov started to punch with his left but stalled, unwilling to let loose his precious jar of balsamic dip.

That moment was just enough time for Arlie to taser him.

Zzzt!

Clank. Clink-clink-clink.

The jar hit the tiled floor, exploding into a shiny forest of pointed shards, the small amount of remaining liquid splattered like spilled coffee.

"My sweet, sweet brown juice," he moaned. Yakov looked up at Arlie as he secured his other hand. "Why you ruin perfect drink?"

Arlie shook his head and started reading him his Miranda rights.

Eddie stepped onto the threshold, her Eddie III drone in hand. "Got everything under control, Arlie?"

Louie stepped out from behind her, stunned and wordless. He made sure the lusty murderer was under control, then moved back, out of Yakov's sight.

"Yeah, but you might want to hang around a while." Arlie nodded toward where Louie had just looked out. "Just to be sure.

Plus, I have a feeling more people will be showing up to this fiasco soon."

Beep. Beep.

Arlie couldn't see beyond the doorway blocked by Eddie and Louie, but he didn't need to. He recognized the horn. Even if she hadn't announced her arrival, Arlie was expecting her.

"A little late to the party, aren't you, Winifred?"

"No, I'm just in time," she said, making her way forward as Louie and Eddie moved back to let her in.

Winifred chuckled, enjoying the superior position of lording over the downed man, even if she couldn't stand on her own two feet. "Well, well, well. If it isn't my old friend Yakov Putin, the KGB-evicted sludge. Looks like you put on a bit of extra weight there, Putin. Oh, and did you get a little reconstructive surgery on that nose? It seems to me that I broke it for you at least twice."

Still on the floor, Yakov lifted his head at the taunt. He squinted and looked through bloodshot, drunken eyes. He recognized her voice but not the stance.

Or lack of one.

"Who are you? You sound like Mary Hatta, spy from good old days, but you are wrinkled. And broken."

Yakov brought up his bound hands and squirmed into a seated position, trying for a better look.

The sudden movement startled Winifred, but she held her position and didn't back up.

Yakov watched the woman on the handicap motor unit flinch at his change in posture and felt emboldened. "Mata Hari or Mary Hatta or someone else." He stuck out his bottom lip in thought. "Still bitch."

Louie turned around and saw three state trooper vehicles pull in. He held onto Eddie's elbow for reassurance and said, "Your ride's here, Yakov."

Four big men walked up, shackles and cuffs clanging from their belts. A fifth officer stayed back. He was examining the roof of Yakov's silver Mercedes sedan. He scraped his fingernail across the top, then lifted what looked like a bird dropping from it. He peered at it, wiped it on his shirt, then put it in his wallet. "For the next time."

"Hey, Andy," Arlie called out. "Boy or girl?"

"Still don't know. It was a false alarm, or I wouldn't be here. I'm sure glad you gave me this little jewel. Looks like we have one more bad guy off the streets because of it."

"I hope so." Arlie looked at Winifred, now backing away from the group. Her face was blank, totally devoid of emotion.

One trooper whispered to Arlie, "You do realize you're out of your jurisdiction."

"Uh-huh. I just came by to check on my neighbor." He nodded to Louie. "I hadn't heard from him in a while and was worried."

"Hey, Arlie," Louie said. "Yeah, it's a good thing you did come by. This guy was spooking me."

"Did he threaten you?" the trooper asked.

"No, but he kept getting real close to me," Louie said. He looked at Yakov. The troopers were assisting him into the backseat of a cruiser. Even though he was subdued, and chances of him escaping or hurting him were minimal, Louie was still afraid of him. His adrenaline was spent. All he wanted was to get home and snuggle Jess and LuLu.

"No, he didn't threaten me," Louie repeated.

"Just the same, we need to get a statement from you."

"Why?" Louie asked. "I just want to go home and hold my daughter. He just scared me real bad, okay?"

"Well, young man, you're lucky. This man is wanted in several states for a long list of felonies. Hurting people is one of them."

"Muh…murder, too?"

The trooper nodded. "We'll call you if we have any questions. Your friend Arlie knows how to get in touch with you, right?"

"Yeah, we're neighbors."

He patted Louie on the shoulder. "Yeah, very lucky…" he repeated as he walked away.

Arlie came over to stand by Louie as half of the troopers departed, the rest staying back to tape off the area. "You know, Louie, I almost lost everything I had by going into a situation I thought I could handle myself."

"Yeah, how could I forget. I saved your life that night, remember?"

"As you say, how could I forget? You were lucky back then, not only in name. You're lucky now in only one way. Don't go gambling with your life, though." Arlie looked at Winifred. "Or let others gamble with it. You have a daughter and a fiancé now. Even a man with the biggest heart ever can be wiped out with one little swish,"

Arlie mimed a throat slit.

"Or a stab," Louie said, looking at Winifred. "Why'd she let me do that, Arlie? She knew better. I could have been killed."

"She wasn't thinking straight, Louie. She was blinded by grief. If something happened to LuLu or Jess, you wouldn't be very rational, either. Would you?"

Louie gasped at the thought. "Oh, man. I really shouldn't have listened to her. And he did confess to me, Arlie. I was right – sorta – about how Nero was murdered. They weren't ice bullets, but he did use an ice sword. Nero was stabbed with an icicle."

Arlie nodded, listening, but still looking at Winifred. He turned back at Louie. "If you testified, Louie, your Witness Protection status would be compromised. You'd have to relocate. You might be able to take LuLu with you, but you're not married right now. What would happen to Jess? He's FBI. I don't know if he'd give up his career to be with you or not. Well, I think he would, but you don't want to put him in that position. And then there's Rita and Charlene and the boys…"

Arlie saw tears welling in Louie's eyes.

"What I'm trying to say – and doing such a lousy job of – is you did right."

"Huh? I thought I made a dumb mistake coming out here, trying to get Yakov to confess to Nero's murder."

"Well, that part was truly idiotic, but you were listening to an authoritarian figure who was judgmentally compromised," Arlie said, looking at Winifred.

"Huh?"

"You listened to a messed-up smart person."

"Oh, yeah. So, what did I do right?"

"You didn't say anything to the troopers about Yakov confessing to the murder. You're not a witness to it, nor do you have any evidence needed to convict Yakov."

"Okay." Louie squinted as he thought. "But how come they took Yakov? All he did was get drunk and try to have his way with me. Or at least, that's what I thought he had in mind..."

"Well, you see, you were wearing that cute little hat that Winifred gave you," Arlie said and winked.

"Oh, yeah!" Louie tapped the hat still on his head.

Winifred had been eavesdropping on everything Arlie and Louie were saying through her fake hearing aid that was synched to Louie's hat. At Louie's, 'Oh, yeah,' she realized she had to interrupt the impending celebration.

"Excuse me," she said, rolling her scooter to a stop between the two.

"Yes..." Arlie and Louie chorused, both smiling.

"It didn't work," she said.

"Wait. What?" Louie asked.

"The uplink failed. I thought it had a longer reach but the mountain or something else was in the way. I didn't get it. I'm sorry, Louie, but I put your life in danger for nothing." Winifred sniffed and bit her bottom lip, then lost it. Tears and shudders began. "He...he...gets away with murder," she stammered.

"No, he doesn't," Eddie said.

"Huh?" Winifred asked.

Arlie chuckled. "You know, you sound just like my sons when you say that."

"Now I'm confused," Winifred said, looking at Eddie, then Arlie, then back again.

"You didn't think you got to have all the fun, did you?" Eddie asked.

Winifred threw both hands in the air. "Would someone explain to me how Yakov is going to be convicted of murder without fingerprints, a murder weapon, any witnesses, video surveillance footage, or a confession?"

Eddie took out her phone and used it to bring Eddie III in for a perfect landing in front of her. She handed it to Louie. "Hold her for a sec, would you?"

Louie nodded. He lifted it up and looked underneath, then held it close. "Okay. No claws on this eagle, right?"

"You got it." Eddie turned back to the others. "I knew if Winifred posted the information online, her previous professional experience would be exposed. Arlie couldn't do it because he's a cop and didn't have a warrant."

"Hey, it wasn't my device," Arlie said. "Oops. Sorry. Go ahead, Eddie."

"I took a little liberty and hacked into Arlie's hack into Louie's hat. I fed the information directly to an anonymous account that monitors criminal activity around the world. Oh, and to a popular

YouTube channel. What went on in that motel room was posted as a live feed to the world, Louie."

"Wha…What…" Louie kept hold of the Eddie III drone with one hand but grabbed his ballcap with the other, shoving it under his armpit to stop any more live transmissions.

"Don't worry. As soon as it got crowded in here with troopers, the feed stopped. I can repost it again, if you'd like, Louie." Eddie looked at her phone. "Looks like you already have over twenty thousand hits."

"Can you take it down?" Louie asked.

"Yeah, I can archive it, but the information is still out there."

"Archive it. I don't want anyone else to almost recognize me." Louie looked at Arlie. "Do you think that would work?"

Arlie nodded to Eddie. "Better safe than sorry. Yakov's comrades probably monitor that criminal activity site. He won't get another contract. As a matter of fact, if he gets out of the murder rap on a technicality, there's still the counterfeiting charge."

"Huh?" Louie asked. He pulled out the four one-hundred-dollar bills Yakov had paid him for the bread and dip. "And here I was going to give half of this to you, Winifred. Geez, lady. It looks like we both lose on this one."

Winifred reached over and took back the one loaf of unopened Mount Spurr Sourdough bread. "Mostly," she said. "But at least we know who did it and how."

Chapter 17: Audio Specialist or Audio Genius?

Abby's Lab

"I'm sorry but Arlie's not here," Abby told the receptionist via the video link.

"Hold on a sec," the front desk lady said. "I think you need to talk to him." She handed the very young man a portable smartphone. "Here's Abby. Maybe she can help you."

"I'm sorry but Arlie's not here," Abby repeated.

"He told me he had a big challenge," the teenage boy said. "He said if I solved it, he'd give me a great recommendation for early admittance into the forensics program at the university."

"Who are you and how old are you?" Abby asked.

"I'm Zach Pietz, and it's not nice to ask a person their age, no matter what gender."

"*Touché.*" Abby's eyes opened wide. "Hey, are you the audio specialist?"

"Arlie says I'm an audio genius but yeah, audio specialist works, too. Normally, I'd be able to do my work with a digital file, but since the device is damaged, I might have to do it hands-on. Are you able to help me or do I have to wait for Arlie? I do have places to go, you know."

Abby cleared her throat, wondering if his other 'places to go' were skateboard parks or video arcades. "I'll be right there."

Zach ended the call and handed the phone to the receptionist. "Not bad, but I can upgrade the video to 3D if you want."

"Oh, no. No thank you. I don't want to get any closer to some of these callers than I have to. Audio only is good enough for me."

"Okay. Just let me know." He pulled a card out of his pocket and handed it to her. "Or give me a call, just because. You're kinda cute."

"Hey, hey, hey," Abby blurted out, overhearing the last part of the conversation. "I don't know about you, Zach, but we're all adults here. Treat every woman like you'd want others to treat your mother, okay?"

Zach gasped. "Shoot." He looked at the lady behind the desk. "I'm sorry. I never thought of it that way. I guess skipping a few grades really did mess with learning social skills." He took a step closer to her and whispered, "I really am sorry."

The thirty-ish woman giggled and blushed. "Forgiven."

"Come on, Romeo," Abby said, pulling him away by the elbow. "I helped you, now you help me. And you'll never get beyond the first week of cop school if you don't wise up in the real world."

"Gotcha."

Abby brought Zach into her office and set the tray with the quarter-sized camera on it in front of him. "Before you get started on that, here's the audio we want cleared up."

She moved the mouse and opened the audio file. A faint scratching sound came through.

"Do you hear that, just after the footsteps? It sounds like it could be chatter."

Zach turned his head toward the speaker and closed his eyes, listening for two minutes as a barely audible noise came through the speaker. He finally spoke up. "Yup. It's a conversation between two men. One of them is Russian or Ukrainian, I'd say. The other is from the Midwest – Chicago, maybe."

"Wait. You can hear that in those little scratchy noises? Without even using headphones? And you won't need to tear apart the camera?"

"Yeah, well, some folks have perfect pitch. I have that plus can hear ultrasonic sounds. It's both a blessing and a curse. Now, if you have an oscilloscope and the audio files of your suspects, I can work my magic and amplify what you played on this," he pointed to her computer, "to hear exactly what they're saying."

Abby held up one finger. "I'm going to make a call. Don't say a word."

Abby's fingers flew over her keyboard as she opened a new audio file and dialed the morgue. "Hey, Manny. I forgot to ask you something. Remember when you sort of flirted with me a few days ago? Tell me where you wanted to go and what you wanted to do. I'm curious."

"Well, darling," Manny started, "I wanted to take you out to dinner first. You know, start with shrimp cocktails and a few bottles of white wine. Then, if you're in the mood for Italian, I know a great restaurant in Chicago. We can catch a direct flight and get there just as the action starts around midnight. After a few pre-dinner cocktails, we'll switch to red wine and pasta. Veal *parmigiana* and *cannelloni*…

Mm-wah!"

Abby stifled a groan at hearing Manny pucker up and make a kissing sound. She swallowed her pride and asked, "Hey, but what if I want Russian food? I'd like to try something different."

"All Russian food is *diermo*. It tastes like shit," Manny huffed, then realized something was wrong. "Hey, why are you hitting on me? I thought you were a lesbian."

"Oh, that's right. I am. Sorry, I'll have to pass. I suppose I'm just not that curious. See ya!"

Click!

Abby shut off the recording and looked at Zach. "Was that enough?"

"Yup. I'm pretty sure he's a match for the Midwest guy. I'll run it through the 'scope and digitize it for the record. I still need a sound file for the other one. Damn! This Manny guy's Russian accent is spot on. I'd say he grew up speaking it. Oops. Sorry about the cussing."

Abby giggled at his sudden chauvinism, then got back to work. She tapped, clicked, and opened the recording of Yakov's rant at Dolly's Midtown Bakery. "How about this?"

Zach's chagrin changed into a very satisfied smile. "And here I thought this was going to be a challenge. No hunting required. You brought these guys right to me. All I need to do is pluck a few feathers, and these geese are ready to cook."

"Huh?"

"May I?" Zach asked, nodding to her spot at the computer.

"Yeah, sure." Abby got up and let him have her chair.

Zach pulled a thumb drive out of his pocket and plugged it into the computer console. "Just a second…" The mouse zipped across the monitor as he opened recent files, dragged, and then dropped them into his program. The two of them watched wordlessly as the progress bar crawled along, taking an extra moment to go from ninety-nine to one hundred percent.

"Done!" Zach said, arms up like he'd just got the highest score on the video game. "Are you ready to hear this?"

"Actually, no. Let me get in touch with Arlie and see if he wants to hear this first with us."

Abby sent a quick text. 'Can U call me?'

Dum-dum… dum-dee-dum!

"Is that Iron Man by Ozzy?" Zach asked, hearing the personalized ringtone.

Abby nodded and answered the phone. "Hey, Arlie. I'm putting you on speaker. Your buddy Zach Pietz is here with me. He really is an audio genius."

"Hey, Pizza Tech! Thanks for stopping by. I just wrapped this up here in Wasilla. Unless you found something incriminating, all we have new on Yakov is passing funny money."

"Oh, I think you're gonna like this. I don't know if it's admissible or not but probably. This is the surveillance camera you found near the site of the murder, though, right? The one from victim's property?"

"Yup. Brighten my day, kid."

Zach clicked on the file, and they all listened to the cleaned-up, enhanced version.

"What you want, sassy boy?"

"I come to make a deal. I know what you did just over there. I'm not sure how you did it, but I'm the coroner in this mosquito-infested mess of a state. I have evidence right here that can convict you."

"I only not kill you because you are my sister's son."

"Not because I'm the one who called you and told you I found Sonny? Come on, Uncle Yakov. Sonny or Nero or Smiley – whatever you want to call the rat – you said you'd pay a million bucks to anyone who gave you a solid lead. Well, I did. I don't care one way or another if you killed him or not. If you did, you're safe. I have a lot of clout as a coroner."

"You destroy cheek swabs and other body samples?"

"Well, yes and no."

"Do not tell me yes or no. Either you did or did not."

"I did a little misdirection. Plus, in case there's a problem with the assistant coroner, I have her thinking there's a ghost involved. A little light flickering and thumps in the hall, and she's willing to believe in spooks."

"Good. Now I not have to pay you. You do it for family, da?"

"Nope. Hey, I'm an American now. At least, I look and sound like one. That means I'm a capitalist. Just like you, I don't do freebies. I know you have the bucks. Don't be so cheap. Two hundred grand is chump change for you. I just want enough for a nice motor home and a little spending money. Oh, and a good reference spread around locally would be appreciated. You know, for a small fee, prime

evidence from the coroner's office can be lost or switched around?"

Yakov chuckled. "Da. I give you two-hundred big bucks, plus a bonus for being so clever. I let everyone know what you do, too. You just like your momma. You look clean but think dirty."

"Okay. Here's what I want you to do. Box up the money and send it by courier to my house. I'll text you the information. After that, you probably won't ever hear from me again."

"Okay."

"And thanks in advance."

"You welcome in advance, too."

The sound of one set of footsteps walking away came through until it faded away.

"I never like my sister and I never like you. Get ready for big trouble, nephew."

Clip. Clop. Clip. Clop. Uneven footsteps, as if the person had a limp, came closer and closer until...

Crunch!

Zach hit stop. "Done."

Arlie asked, "That's it, then?"

"I'm afraid so," Zach said. "I'd say the Russian dude stepped on the camera as he walked away. I might be able to get more if I messed with the device itself, but from what I heard, you probably have enough."

"I think you're right. Thanks for your help. I'll be in touch. Oh, and Abby, once you two are done, give me another call. I think you'll be able to take all your ladies' room notes down soon. Very soon."

"Will do. And thanks."

Abby ended the call and turned to Zach. "Pizza Tech? I thought you were an audio tech."

Zach shook his head. "It's my name scrambled – the letters of Zach Pietz rearranged. That, and I make a mean pineapple, mango, and pepperoni pizza with sourdough crust." He winked at her. "Maybe I can interest you in dinner and dessert in one dish?"

"Only if I can bring my wife," Abby said and winked back.

"Oh? Oh, yeah. That's right. That's why you weren't interested in Manny."

"I'd never be interested in a creep like Manny. Tone done the flirts, Zach. You'll get more romantic leads with mystic than macho." Abby patted him on the shoulder and added. "You don't need a strong come on. You're a cool dude just as you are. Don't spoil it."

***

Jess showed off his delivery service uniform and his See-Hawks hat. "How do I look?"

Arlie chuckled. "Like you could get a job there anytime you got tired of the FBI. Good work intercepting the package."

"I can't believe Manny was so stupid and gave Yakov his work address to send the cash to."

"I don't think he did. I think Yakov sent it there to set him up. Payola is payola, whether it's real money or counterfeit. Ready?"

"The trackers are in place. Once he takes it home and keeps it in his possession for twenty-four hours or spends even one c-note, he's done. He won't be able to claim he was going to turn it over as evidence. Sometimes it feels great to ruin someone's day."

"Yes, it does. One less scum on the streets."

"Or in the back offices of government agencies."

"Ten-four."

DENOUEMENT

Winifred took her worn, black leather clutch from of the basket of her scooter and pulled the coffee-stained envelope from it. She opened it and inhaled. A residual aroma of Nero lingered: yeasty and earthy at the same time, just like him.

She removed the Polaroid snapshot of a dandelion and the note written on notebook paper. She wiped away tears as she read it again.

My dearest Winifred,

Please accept my small token of beauty and words of encouragement for you. Unlike the real thing, this photo of a dandelion will last forever. Winter snow and summer heat won't dim its brilliance.

An obnoxious weed to many, to me dandelions are a promise from God. Although winter can be bleak – especially here in Alaska – brighter, 'golden' days are ahead. Despite adversity, they will not only survive, but they will also thrive.

Unconquerable. Unstoppable. Just like you.

If you can only hold on a little bit longer, I'll give you beauty as you've never seen it. I've sold the bakery, sourdough starter, and all my recipes. I'll no longer be tethered to my little half-acre in the woods. Just give me this one last summer season, then you and I can travel the world.

Together we can gather images of flowers and natural wonders. In deserts and rainforests, on mountaintops and beaches, wherever planes, trains, and pedicabs go, we'll share their beauty. Their inspiration. Their heart.

Although we can travel as you are now, I implore you to get the back surgery. We'll be able to walk, swim, and have other fun (grin) without constraint.

Cost is no longer an obstacle. I know for you the procedure involves a lot of therapy, and maybe a bit of pain, but we both know it's time to have it done. You need to do it for you, though, not me. I'll love you forever, whether you're running marathons or in a hospital bed with tubes and wires keeping you alive. But I'd rather see you healthy.

Who knows how much time we have left? Regardless of whether you're on your ruby red scooter or skipping beside me in bright white tennis shoes, let's spend those days together.

And once again, I'd rather do it as husband and wife.
Yours forever.
Love,
'Nero'

Winifred sniffed the paper one more time, then folded it on its original lines and put it and the snapshot back in the envelope.

"I guess it's time," she said as she returned the envelope to her small purse. "I'll make the call. I'm tired of asking others to do my job.

221

"It's time to stand on my own two feet."

The End

Afterword

Thank you for reading NEVER A DULL MURDER, part of the ARLIE UNDERCOVER series.

Writing this story was a blast! If you had half as much fun reading it as I did creating it, then it's a success.

If you could take a moment to leave an honest review on Amazon, I'd appreciate it. Authors love even short reviews about what their readers liked about their stories.

If you want to know more about Arlie, Charlene, Chip and Carlos, Louie, Jess, and the rest, check out the rest of the series. Start with A STINGRAY CHRISTMAS. Arlie takes a medical leave and finds more in Arizona than he expected. Good clean action adventure and a bit of romance.

My website www.danihaviland.com has my books and box sets listed with descriptions and links of where to purchase them. A few are even FREE! You can also sign up for my newsletter there.

Read on!

Other Books from the Author

I have written *dozens* of books. Rather than list them all here, check out my website. Here are the major series, plus I also have many Stand-Alone singles available.

LOST: The Time Travel Romance That Started It All (https://Books2Read.com/losttimetravel) is my gift to readers. If you like parodies and satires, you might like this 'poke' at the outlandish fans of a popular time travel series. This book is also an introduction to a few major characters in THE FAIRIES SAGA and ARLIE UNDERCOVER series.

THE FAIRIES SAGA (historical fiction and time travel romance) is where it all began. I suggest starting this series with AYE, I AM A FAIRY. (www.danihaviland.com/the-fairies-saga/)

ARLIE UNDERCOVER (clean romantic suspense and cozy mysteries with LGBTQ leads in the later books). From Alaska to Arizona and back again, Arlie is finding friends and a new family along the way while thwarting bad guys and protecting the good ones. (www.danihaviland.com/arlie-undercover)

TRIPLETS: THREE AREN'T ONE (mixed genres including women's fiction and romantic comedy with a few LGBTQ leads) Grace was told her babies had died, so tried to get on with her life. What started as tragedy winds up one of the best Happy Ever Afters possible for everyone involved. (www.danihaviland.com/the-triplets-are-coming)

THAT TWIN THING (romantic suspense) The midwife took the unwanted twin to bring up as her own. Years later, the two young men meet under strained situations, neither one of them knowing the other existed. Redemption, forgiveness, and Happy Ever Afters with a few surprises. (www.danihaviland.com/that-twin-thing)

ASSORTED STAND-ALONE STORIES (from clean to slightly spicy and many different genres). Printed books and stand-alone e-books (that are not in a series) are also available. Check here: http://danihaviland.com/The-Singles-and-Large-Print-Formats/

About the Author

Author Dani Haviland started writing late in life and has been making up for lost time with a flood of works from parodies to romantic comedies to historical romances to romantic suspense and cozy mysteries.

Dani is also the owner of Chill Out! Books, one of the publishers for The Authors' Billboard (http://bit.ly/MGABB)

Follow her on Amazon: (http://bit.ly/dhAuthor) and BookBub (http://bit.ly/BBDani)_to make sure you get her latest stories.

Contact information:

Website www.danihaviland.com

Facebook: https://www.facebook.com/ChillOutDani

BookBub: http://bit.ly/BBDani

Goodreads: http://bit.ly/2DHgdrds

Email: dani@danihaviland.com

Twitter: @dani_haviland

www.ingramcontent.com/pod-product-compliance
Lightning Source LLC
Chambersburg PA
CBHW051947220626
47052CB00004B/836